It couldn't be too comfortable for Adam to carry her son, with those metal braces bumping against his chest, but it didn't deter him.

Adam was looking up at Jamie, laughing at something, and the expression on Jamie's face made Cathy's heart stop.

A fierce longing swept through her to have that for Jamie—a strong man to carry him on his shoulder, to make him laugh, to show him how to grow up into a good man.

She pushed the thought away just as fiercely. It wasn't likely to happen. Just look at how Adam had reacted, stepping away so quickly after he'd kissed her. That should tell her all she needed to know.

But there was *more* to know.

Books by Marta Perry

Love Inspired

*Hunter's Bride
*A Mother's Wish
*A Time To Forgive
*Promise Forever
Always in Her Heart
The Doctor's Christmas
True Devotion
**Hero in Her Heart
**Unlikely Hero
**Hero Dad
**Her Only Hero

**Hearts Afire
**Restless Hearts
**A Soldier's Heart
Mission: Motherhood
†Twice in a Lifetime
†Heart of the Matter
†The Guardian's Honor

*Caldwell Kin
**The Flanagans
†The Bodine Family

Love Inspired Suspense

Tangled Memories
Season of Secrets
‡Hide in Plain Sight
‡A Christmas to Die For

‡Buried Sins
Final Justice
Twin Targets

‡The Three Sisters Inn

MARTA PERRY

has written everything from Sunday school curricula to travel articles to magazine stories in more than twenty years of writing, but she feels she's found her writing home in the stories she writes for the Love Inspired lines.

Marta lives in rural Pennsylvania, but she and her husband spend part of each year at their second home in South Carolina. When she's not writing, she's probably visiting her children and her six beautiful grandchildren, traveling, gardening or relaxing with a good book.

Marta loves hearing from readers, and she'll write back with a signed bookmark and/or her brochure of Pennsylvania Dutch recipes. Write to her c/o Steeple Hill Books, 233 Broadway, Suite 1001, New York, NY 10279, e-mail her at marta@martaperry.com, or visit her on the Web at www.martaperry.com.

The Guardian's Honor
Marta Perry

Steeple
Hill®

Published by Steeple Hill Books™

STEEPLE HILL BOOKS

Steeple
Hill®

Recycling programs
for this product may
not exist in your area.

ISBN-13: 978-0-373-81485-5

THE GUARDIAN'S HONOR

Copyright © 2010 by Martha Johnson

www.SteepleHill.com

Printed in U.S.A.

Bear with one another and forgive whatever grievances you may have against one another. Forgive as the Lord forgave you.

—*Colossians* 3:13

This story is dedicated to Bill and Molly Perry, my dear brother and sister-in-law. And, as always, to Brian, with much love.

Chapter One

"What are you doing?" The woman's soft Georgia drawl bore a sharp edge of hostility.

Adam Bodine took a step back on the dusty lane and turned toward the woman with what he hoped was a disarming smile. "Just admiring your garden, ma'am."

Actually, the garden *was* worthy of a second glance. By early September at the tail end of a hot, dry summer, most folks would find their tomato plants shriveled to a few leafless vines, but these still sported fat red tomatoes.

The woman rose from where she'd been kneeling, setting a basket of vegetables on the ground, the movement giving him a better look at her.

She was younger than he'd thought in that first quick glance. A faded ball cap covered blond hair pulled back in a ponytail, its brim shielding her eyes so that he couldn't see what color they were. Light, he thought. Her slim shoulders were stiff under a faded, oversized plaid shirt, giving the impression that she braced herself for something unpleasant. Was that habitual, or did his appearance account for it?

"These tomatoes are about ready to give up," she said, still guarded. "Did you want something?"

He did, but it was far better if this woman didn't know what had brought him to the ramshackle farm deep in the Georgia mountains. At least, not until he knew for sure he was in the right place.

"Just passing by." He glanced back down the winding lane that had brought him to what he hoped was the last stop on a long hunt. *Please, Lord.* "I don't suppose you get many strangers up here."

"No." The tone said she didn't want any, either. "Look, if you're sellin' something…"

A chuckle escaped him. "Do I look like a salesman?" He spread his hands, inviting her to assess him.

There wasn't much he could do to make his six-foot frame less intimidating, but he tried to ease his military bearing and relax his face into the smile that his sister always said was at its most boyish when he was up to something. At least the jeans, T-shirt, and ball cap he wore were practically a uniform these days.

"Maybe not a salesman," she conceded. "But

you haven't explained what you're doing on a private road." She sent a quick, maybe worried glance toward the peeling white farmhouse that seemed to doze in the afternoon heat. "Mr. Hawkins doesn't like visitors."

Mr. Hawkins. The formal address might mean she wasn't a relative. A caregiver, maybe?

"Actually, I'm looking for someone. A man named Ned Bodine. Edward Bodine, to be exact." He studied her as he said the words, looking for any sign of recognition.

The woman took the ball cap off, frowning as she wiped her forehead with the sleeve of the plaid shirt, leaving a streak of dirt she probably hadn't intended. Her eyes were light, as he'd supposed, neither blue nor green but hazel. That heart-shaped face might have been pretty if not for whatever it was that tightened it—worry, maybe, or just plain dislike of nosy strangers.

"Sorry," she said. "I don't believe I've ever heard the name. Now, if you'll excuse me…" She gestured toward the garden.

"You're sure?" Of course she might not know, even if she were a relative of his great-uncle. Ned Bodine had stayed missing for sixty-some years, which meant he probably kept his secrets well.

"That's what I said, isn't it?" She snapped the words at him, picking up the basket as if it were a shield.

So much for getting anything out of her. "In that case, I'd like to speak to Mr. Theodore Hawkins."

She gave him a wary, suspicious stare. "Why?"

"Look, I don't blame you for being cautious, Ms...."

"Mrs.," she corrected. "Mrs. Norwood." She bit off the words, as if regretting giving him that much.

The name wasn't the same, but that didn't mean she couldn't be related. She could be...let's see, what was it? Second or third cousin, maybe?

"I know it seems odd, having a perfect stranger coming along and asking questions, but I do need to talk with Mr. Hawkins."

"He's resting right now. He always takes a rest in the afternoon. He's not to be disturbed."

The way she phrased that made it sound as it she took orders from the man. Probably not a relative, then, so he had to be stingy with what he told her. Gossip flew fast in country places, even though there wasn't another house in sight.

"Look, I think he'd probably be willing to talk with me." Doubt assailed him as he said the words. What made him think Ned Bodine wanted to be found after all these years? Still, all he could do was try. "Just tell him Adam Bodine wants to see him. Please."

He glanced toward the house, hoping to see some

sign of life. Nothing, but he noticed something he hadn't before. A child played under the shade of a tall pine near the corner of the porch, running toy cars in the dirt.

"Your little boy?" he asked. Maybe an expression of interest in her child would ease the ice between them.

His words seemed to have the opposite effect. She moved, putting herself into position to block his view of the child.

"I told you. Mr. Hawkins is resting. He wouldn't be able to help you, anyway."

"We won't know that until we ask him, will we?" He put a little steel into the words. Obviously this Mrs. Norwood wasn't going to fall victim to the notorious Bodine charm. "When can I see him?"

She clamped her lips together for a long moment. She could either give in, or she could threaten to call the sheriff on him. Which would it be?

Finally she gave a curt nod. "All right. Come back tonight around six." She gave a pointed look from him to his car.

Nobody would say he couldn't take a hint. "Thank you, ma'am. I'll be back at six."

She didn't respond, bending again to her tomato plants as if he weren't there.

He gave the sleeping house a final glance. He'd be back. With any luck, this long search would end here.

* * *

Cathy cleared the supper dishes quickly, half her attention on the clock. Somehow she hadn't managed to tell her grandfather yet about the visitor, and the man would be here in minutes.

She slanted a glance at her grandfather. He was whittling a soft piece of pine, turning it into a boat for her son. Six-year-old Jamie sat next to him, elbows on the table, his blue eyes fixed on the boat as it emerged from the wood.

A smile softened her lips. Grandpa had done the same for her as a child, creating fanciful animals and even small dolls. She'd been as close to him then as Jamie was now, and she'd never have dreamed that could change.

But it had. Her mind winced away from the bitter memory.

Grandpa and Jamie were the only family she had, but her willfulness had created a seemingly unbreakable wall between her and her stepgrandfather.

As for Jamie—her heart swelled with love for her son. Jamie needed so much, more than she could possibly provide unless things changed.

Her mind went round and round, back on the familiar track. She had to take care of her grandfather. She had to provide the surgery and therapy her son needed. How? How would she do that?

She suddenly realized that Jamie's prattle about

the game he'd been playing with his toy cars had turned in a new direction.

"…and he drove a silver car, and Mama said he should come back to talk to you."

Grandpa's gaze swiveled to hers, his bushy white brows drawing down over his eyes. "What's all this, then, Cathleen? Who was here? Somebody selling something?"

She wiped her hands on the dish towel. "He said he was looking for information about someone. Someone he thought you might know, apparently. A man named Edward Bodine."

Grandpa's hand slipped on the carving, and the half-finished boat dropped to the floor. For an instant silence seemed to freeze the old farmhouse kitchen.

Then he shoved himself to his feet, grabbing his cane. "I won't see him." His face reddened. "You know how I feel about strangers. Tell him to go away."

She quaked inside at the anger in his tone, but then her own temper rose. She wouldn't let him bully her. She glanced past him, out the kitchen window.

"You can tell him yourself. He's just pulled up." She touched her son's shoulder. "Jamie, you go play in your room for a bit."

Without waiting for a response, she walked away, reaching the door as she heard the man's footsteps on the creaky porch. She opened the door before the knock could sound.

Bodine looked a little startled, but he recovered quickly. Not the sort to be rattled easily, she'd think. Tall, with a bearing that said military and the kind of strong-boned face that would compel obedience.

For just an instant she thought she glimpsed something bleak behind the brown eyes, and then his face relaxed in an easy, open smile.

"Mrs. Norwood. I hope I'm not too early."

"It's fine." At least, she hoped it was. It was hard to tell how rude her grandfather intended to be. On the other hand, this man looked capable of handling just about anything Grandpa could throw at him. "Please, come in."

Adam Bodine stepped into the house, wiping his feet on the threadbare rug by the door. "Thank you for seeing me."

He wasn't looking at her. Instead, he stared over her shoulder at her grandfather with an expression in his eyes she couldn't quite make out. It was almost a look of recognition.

"This is Theodore Hawkins," she said.

"Adam Bodine." He held out his hand, smiling.

Grandpa ignored it, his face tight and forbidding. "Whatever it is you want, I'm not interested. You can be on your way."

She sucked in a breath, but Bodine didn't seem fazed by the blunt words.

"I need to talk with you, sir. About my great-uncle, Edward Bodine." He paused, glancing at her. "Maybe we should do this in private."

It took an instant to realize that he must think she was just the hired help. Well, maybe that wasn't far from the truth.

"You can talk in front of me," she said. "This is my grandfather."

"Stepgrandfather," Grandpa said.

She wouldn't let him see how much it hurt to hear it said aloud. It was true, of course. Her mother had been his stepdaughter, not his daughter. Still, he'd never referred to her that way, probably never even thought about it, before she'd gone away.

There was still a trace of hesitation in Bodine's face, but he nodded. "Fine. As I said, I've come here to ask about Ned Bodine, my grandfather's older brother. He disappeared in 1942."

"Disappeared?" Her grandfather wasn't responding, so apparently it was up to her. "What do you mean? Disappeared how?"

Bodine switched his focus to her. "He ran away from the family home on Sullivan's Island. Near Charleston?" He made it a question.

"I know where Sullivan's Island is." One of the barrier islands off Charleston, the kind of place where people with money built summer houses, she'd guess. "Why did he run away?" He'd said 1942. "Does this have something to do with the war?"

Her grandfather never talked about the war, but he'd served then. She remembered hearing her grandmother say something to her mother about it, and then turning to her eight-or-nine-year-old self and cautioning her not to mention it.

He doesn't want to talk about the war, so we have to respect that. Her grandmother's soft voice had seemed very mournful. *It did bad things to him.*

"People said Ned ran away because he was afraid to fight in the war," Bodine said. "We—the family, that is—we're sure that's not true."

Her grandfather turned away. With one hand he gripped the back of a straight chair, his grasp so hard that the veins stood out of the back of his hand.

Tension edged along Cathy's skin like a cold breeze. Something was wrong. Something about this man's words affected Grandpa. She shook her head, trying to shake off the tension.

"I don't understand what this has to do with us. Are you saying my grandfather knew this Ned Bodine?"

"No." He looked from her to her grandfather, seeming to gauge their responses. "I'm saying that your grandfather is Ned Bodine."

The chair Grandpa held skidded against the wood floor as he shoved it. "Get out."

"Grandpa…"

"Stay out of it." He turned to her a face that seemed stripped down to the bone.

"I know this is a shock," Bodine said. "But if we can just talk it over—" He cut the words off suddenly, looking beyond her to the doorway.

She whirled. Jamie stood there, hanging on to the frame with one hand. He swung one leg forward, its brace glinting dully. "Mama, I can't find my bear."

"Not now, Jamie." She moved to him, easing him protectively away from the two tense figures in the living room.

But Jamie craned his neck to see around her, smiling at Adam Bodine. Unlike his great-grand-father, Jamie loved company, and he saw very little of it.

"Hey. I'm Jamie."

"Hey, Jamie." Bodine's response was all right, but his expression wasn't.

Anger welled in her. How dare he look at her child with shock and pity in his eyes? She pulled Jamie a little closer, her arms cradling him.

"You heard my grandfather, Mr. Bodine. It's time for you to leave."

He stared at her for a long moment. Then, without another word, he backed out the door and walked quickly away.

"Was he a bad man, Mama?" Jamie snuggled against his pillows after his good-night prayers, looking up at Cathy with wide, innocent eyes.

Cathy smoothed his blond cowlick with her palm, love tugging at her heart. "No, I'm sure he's not." How to explain to her son something that she didn't understand herself? "He wanted to find out something about a…a friend of his, but Grandpa couldn't help him."

Couldn't? Or wouldn't? Her grandfather's reactions to the Bodine man had been odd, to say the least.

After Bodine left, Grandpa had stalked to his bedroom and slammed the door. He hadn't come out until she was putting Jamie in the tub, and then he'd ignored the subject of their visitor as if the man didn't exist, instead talking to Jamie about his boat and promising to have it finished by bath time the next day.

"But Grandpa would've helped the man if he could've, right, Mama? 'Cause that's what Jesus would want him to do."

"I'm sure he would," she said, though her heart wasn't at all sure.

How difficult it was to teach her son about faith

when her own was as weak as a willow twig. She smoothed the sheet over him and bent to kiss his soft cheek.

"Good night, little man. I love you great big bunches."

His arms squeezed her tightly. "I love you great big bunches, too, Mama."

She dropped another light kiss on his nose and went out, leaving the door ajar. She followed the sound of the refrigerator door opening to the kitchen.

Grandpa was pouring himself a glass of sweet tea. He lifted the pitcher toward her and raised his eyebrows in a question. Taking that as a peace offering, she nodded.

"Some tea sounds good about now. September's turning out near as hot as August, seems like."

He brought the glasses to the table and sank into his usual chair. "Too dry. We'd better not spare any more water for those tomato plants, I reckon, if we want the well to hold out."

It was the sort of conversation that passed for normal now between them. Since she'd come back to the house where she was raised, destitute and with a disabled child in tow, she and Grandpa had existed in a kind of neutral zone, as if they were simply roommates.

Grandpa had been that way with Jamie at first, too, but it hadn't taken long for love to blossom between them. She found joy every day that Jamie now had the father figure who'd been absent from his life.

She had to be content with that and not expect anything for herself. Once Grandpa had made up his mind about someone, he wouldn't turn back.

So she had nothing to lose by pushing him a little about that odd visit. She moved her cold glass, making wet circles on the scrubbed pine tabletop. "What did you make of Adam Bodine?"

His face tightened. "Fellow was just barkin' up the wrong tree, that's all. Maybe he was pulling some kind of scam."

That hadn't occurred to her. She considered it for a moment, and then set it aside.

"He could have been mistaken, maybe, but not a con artist. The man radiated integrity, it seemed to me."

"You're not exactly a great judge of men, now, are you?"

She'd heard that so often that it no longer had the power to hurt. Maybe she was too easily taken in, as Grandpa believed, but she didn't think she was wrong about Adam Bodine.

She also wasn't wrong about her grandfather's reaction to the Bodine name. And their visitor had seemed convinced that he had the right man. But how could Grandpa have a past identity that she knew nothing about?

"Bodine," she said casually, as if it meant nothing at all. "Did you ever hear anything about that family?"

"Nothing," he snapped, but his hand tensed on the glass. "You that anxious to find yourself a new family? Is that it?"

"No, of course not, Grandpa." She reached out to pat his arm, but he pulled it away, nursing his grievance.

Not a new family. No. She'd just like to have back the family she'd once had. There'd been a time when she and Grandpa and Grandma were everything to each other, but that was gone forever. Now Jamie was the only one who loved her unconditionally.

Thinking of him made her glance at the calendar. "Jamie's appointment with Dr. Greener is Thursday. Do you want to go along to town with us?"

"Greener." Grandpa snorted. "Man's no good at all. You oughta take the boy up to Atlanta or someplace where they can fix him."

If it was possible. The spina bifida Jamie had been born with had necessitated what seemed like an endless series of visits to doctors, specialists, surgeons. After the last surgery, the doctor had been optimistic. Maybe another operation would do it. Maybe Jamie could get rid of the braces for good. But that took money—money she didn't have and didn't see any prospect of getting.

"I wish I could." Her throat had tightened so much that the words came out in a whisper.

"Maybe if I sold the house…"

"Then where would we live?" They'd been over this so many times, and the answer always came out the same. She patted his hand quickly, before he could draw away. "Dr. Greener does his best. We'll be all right." She stood. "I'd better make sure Jamie's not in there playing with his cars instead of sleeping."

She went quickly back to Jamie's bedroom, thankful that the old house had enough rooms to sleep all of them on the first floor, so she could be within easy reach of Grandpa and Jamie if they needed her in the night. She eased the door open and crossed to the bed.

Jamie slept curled up on his side, one hand still wrapped around the old metal car Grandpa had found for him in the attic. His long eyelashes made crescents against the delicate shadows under his eyes.

Did Jamie run in his dreams? Did he splash in the creek and chase fireflies in the dusk?

Such small things to be able to give a child, but she couldn't even manage that much.

But if Grandpa was hiding the truth, if he really was one of the Charleston Bodines, what then? Hope hurt, coming at her unexpectedly. If the Bodines really were family, if they cared enough to search out a long-lost relative, maybe they'd be people who wanted to help a child like Jamie if they knew he was kin.

Or maybe there was an inheritance owed to Grandpa all these years. You heard about such things sometimes, folks coming into money they hadn't expected.

It was a possibility she couldn't let slip away. Adam Bodine hadn't looked like a man who'd give up easily. She'd have to hope she was right about that.

Chapter Two

Adam lingered in the coffee shop at the motel the morning after his encounter with the Hawkins family. It was a good thirty miles from their house, but the closest he could find. Frowning, he stared at the cooling coffee in front of him.

What was his next step? His gut instinct said he was right about this. Theodore Hawkins was Ned Bodine. He had to be, or why had he reacted the way he had?

But it went beyond that. He couldn't explain it, but when he'd seen the man, he'd known. Maybe it was true that blood called out to blood. The Bodine strain ran strong. He'd looked in that man's eyes, and he'd seen his grandfather there.

But if Ned Bodine refused to be found…

"Mr. Bodine?"

He glanced up and then shot to his feet at the sight of Hawkins's granddaughter. No, stepgranddaughter.

She must have guessed he'd be at the only motel this small town boasted.

"Mrs. Norwood. I didn't expect to see you here."

Especially not after the way he'd reacted when he'd seen her disabled son. He'd kicked himself all the way back to the motel, but it had been unavoidable. He'd looked at her and the boy and seen the other mother and son, felt the pain…

"I thought we should talk." Her gaze was wary, maybe even a little antagonistic. But at least she was here. The door wasn't entirely closed.

"Please, sit down." He pulled out a chair for her. "I'm glad you've come."

"I'm not sure what good it will do. My grandfather is a very stubborn man."

He was tempted to say it ran in the family, but that was presuming too much. Instead he signaled for the server. "You'll have something to eat, won't you?"

"No. Well, just coffee."

While the server brought cups and a fresh pot, he took the opportunity to study Mrs. Norwood. *Mrs.*, she'd said, but she didn't wear a ring. Divorced? Widowed?

Her hands were roughened, no doubt from that garden where he'd first seen her, but they were delicate and long-fingered. Artistic, he'd say, if he believed physical traits meant talents.

As for the rest, his first impression was strengthened. She wore that air of strain like a heavy coat, weighing her down. Her fine-boned face tensed with it, and it spoke in the lines around her hazel eyes. Life hadn't treated her well, and he had a ridiculous urge to fix that.

"Mrs. Norwood," he began.

But she shook her head. "Cathleen. Cathy, please. After all, if you're right, we're...what? Step-second cousins, I guess."

"I guess." He took a sip of the fresh coffee, trying to clear his mind. This woman could help him, if she wanted to, and the fact that she had driven thirty miles to catch him had to be a good sign.

"Cathy." He smiled, relaxing a little at the encouragement. "Since your grandfather wouldn't listen to what brought me here, will you?"

"I guess that's why I've come." Her hands twisted a little before she seemed to force them to relax. "My grandfather doesn't know. He thinks I came to town for groceries."

"I see."

But he didn't, not really. What kind of relationship did she have with her grandfather? Certainly nothing like the one he'd had with his. Even with the huge tribe of grandkids his three sons had managed to produce, Granddad had still found time to make each of them feel special.

"Did your grandfather send you here to find his brother?" she asked.

"Not exactly. My grandfather died several years ago. My grandmother, Miz Callie, is the one who became convinced that Ned couldn't have done what people thought he had."

"Why? What convinced her of that?"

"She remembered him so well, you see. She had faith in him."

He hesitated, doing some mental editing. There was so much more to the story, but he didn't want to overwhelm her with information.

"At first, the family didn't know anything about it, and when they did find out, there was a lot of fuss because they figured Miz Callie was going to be hurt if he really had run off. But it turned out that Ned had enlisted in the Navy under another name after he became estranged from his father."

Her fingers tightened on the cup, as if that fact hit a nerve. "So he never contacted the family again?"

"No." That was the aspect of the whole thing he just didn't get. He could understand an eighteen-year-old rushing off to enlist under another name. He couldn't understand the man Ned must have become cutting himself off from his family for life.

Cathy shook her head slowly, but she didn't seem to find it as hard to believe as he did. "What convinced you that the man you want is my grandfather?"

In answer, he pulled out the envelope of photographs he'd been carrying around. He slid the reproductions of black and white photos onto the tabletop between them.

"This was the first photo I found of Theodore Hawkins after he enlisted." He shoved the picture of the young PT boat crew across to her. "Can you pick out your grandfather?"

She bent over, studying the images of boys, most long dead, before putting her finger on one face. "That's Grandpa."

He handed her another picture. "And here's one of Ned Bodine, taken that last summer." He'd taken the original photo to a professional lab, not content with his own photo program, sharpening the face until he thought he'd recognize his great-uncle in his sleep.

Cathy let out a long, slow breath. "It surely looks like the same person. But if he has family, why would he deny it?"

"You know your grandfather better than I do. Is he the kind of person who would hold on to a grudge that long?"

A shutter seemed to come down over her face, closing him out.

"Sorry," he said quickly. He needed this woman on his side. "That wasn't very tactful. I meant—"

"I know what you meant, and the answer is that I don't know. Maybe." She seemed to stare into the coffee cup, as if looking for answers there. "Tell me about your family. Why are they so interested in finding him?"

"My grandmother," he said simply. "She's the heart of the family, and she wants this so much. How could we not try to help her? As for the family—well, there's a bunch of us. My grandmother and grandfather had three sons, and they married and had kids. There are eleven of us cousins, all pretty close in age."

Now she just looked stunned, maybe at the thought of acquiring so many relatives at one fell swoop.

"Y'all live in Charleston?"

"In and around. My grandmother has moved out to the family beach house on Sullivan's Island. My sister was up in Atlanta for a while, but she's back now. It seems like whenever one of us goes off for a time, he or she just has to come back. Charleston's home to us."

"Beach house?"

"It's been in the Bodine family for years. In fact, that's where Ned ran away from. The family always moved out to the island every summer from the Charleston house."

She glanced at him, something almost speculative in those hazel eyes, and then looked down again. "You said Ned was your grandfather's older brother?"

He nodded. "About six years between them, I think."

"It sounds… Well, it sounds like a life no one would want to give up. If my grandfather is your kin, I'd think he'd be eager to claim it."

She sounded willing to be convinced, and that was half the battle, surely. He'd better bring up the idea he'd been mulling over.

"Is there any chance your grandfather would open up to you about it?"

Her lips tightened. "I don't know. But if he did, if he really is Edward Bodine, what then? What did you think would happen?"

Something was behind her questions, but he wasn't sure what it was. "Best-case scenario? I hoped he might want to come back to Charleston, for a visit if not to stay. Be a part of the family again. At the least, I guess I'd hope he'd want to be in touch with Miz Callie. It would mean a lot to her."

She was silent for a long moment, looking down so that he couldn't see her eyes. The feeling that she was holding something back intensified.

Finally she looked up. "I don't think it'll help any if I talk to him. Once he gets his back up, it's no sense talking."

Disappointment had a sharp edge. If his

granddaughter couldn't convince him, why would he listen to Adam?

"My grandfather is going to lunch today with a friend. I'll have a look through my grandma's boxes in the attic while he's gone. Maybe there'll be something to show, one way or the other. That's the best I can think of to do."

"That's great." Without thinking about it, he put his hand over hers. And felt a connection, as if something ran from his skin to hers.

She met his eyes, her own wide and startled. Then she snatched her hand away and rose.

"I'll be in touch."

She was gone before he could thank her.

Cathy stood at the window, watching the lane. A glint of silver announced Adam's arrival, and her stomach clenched in protest at what she was about to do.

She glanced down at the object in her hand. Did she have the right to show him what she'd found squirreled away in her grandmother's trunk?

If she did, she was opening up something that could have results she couldn't even imagine. But if she didn't, she was passing up the opportunity to change all their lives for the better. They'd just go on and on the way they were, with the bills mounting and their income dropping, and Jamie would never have a chance to see another specialist.

If she could get a decent job, instead of the part-time work that barely paid enough to keep food on the table… But if she had a full-time job, who would take care of Jamie? Who would be there for Grandpa when he got one of his forgetful spells?

The car pulled up at the gate. Determination hardened in her. From what Adam had said, it sounded like the Bodine family was fairly well-off. Grandpa, whether he wanted to admit it or not, was one of them.

He was probably due something from them, in any event. Shouldn't he have a share in that beach house and whatever other family property there was?

Come to think of it, that queasiness in her stomach was probably her conscience, telling her she was wrong to want this reconciliation for what she might get out of it. She pictured her son's face, and her determination hardened. She wouldn't do this for herself, but she'd do it for him.

A knock sounded on the door, and she went to open it. Everything was going to change. She didn't know where the change would take her, but she'd deal with it, for Jamie's sake.

"Cathy?" Adam stepped inside at her gesture, level brows rising. "You found something?"

She nodded. Grandpa could be back at any moment, so she had to make this fast.

"I found this in one of my grandmother's trunks

in the attic." She handed him the tarnished watch. "Look at the inscription."

He turned it over in his hands, tilting it to the light. "E.B. from Mama and Daddy. 1942." His voice choked on the words. For a long moment he was silent, rubbing his thumb over and over the inscription.

"Is it…does that mean what I think it does?"

He nodded. Cleared his throat. "Ned's parents would have given this to him on his eighteenth birthday. It's a family tradition." He turned his wrist. "I'm still wearing the watch my folks gave me. To A.B. from Mama and Daddy, and the date of my eighteenth birthday."

She let out the breath she'd been holding. "It's true, then. My grandfather really is Ned Bodine."

He nodded, handing the watch back to her slowly, as if reluctant to part with it. "Now all we have to do is get him to admit it."

"He should be back soon. Do you want to stay? If we tackle him together, that might be best."

"You're right. Let's not give him time to think up an argument. I'll wait and call my grandmother afterward. I'd like to have good news for her."

"This means a lot to her." She responded to the message behind the words.

"It's all she's talked about for months." He frowned slightly. "She thought he'd died in the war. She wanted to set up a memorial to him. Once we realized he might still be alive, there was just no containing her. If I hadn't taken on finding him, I think she'd have set out herself." Now his lips curved in a smile that blended affection and exasperation.

It was an appealing smile. She considered herself hardened to the effects of masculine appeal, but there was something about Adam Bodine that seemed to get under her guard.

She gave herself a mental shake. There was no room in her life for thoughts like that.

"I'll just get us some sweet tea. You make yourself comfortable." She escaped to the kitchen.

She'd no sooner put ice in the tea than she heard voices in the living room. Her nerves twitched. If Grandpa was back already…

But that wasn't her grandfather talking to Adam. It was Jamie's piping little voice. Snatching the tray, she hurried back into the room.

Adam sat on the faded sofa, the half-finished wooden boat in his hand. Jamie leaned against his knee.

"My grandfather used to whittle things for me, too. Sea creatures, mostly…dolphins and whales and sea horses. I still have them on a shelf in my bedroom."

"I wish I could see them." Jamie's voice was wistful. "Is your house a long, long way?"

"Not too far," Adam began, but he cut the words off when he saw her.

She set the tray down, keeping her smile intact with an effort. "Jamie, it's time for your snack. Come along to the kitchen now."

"But, Mama, I want to talk to Mr. Adam."

"Not now." She put her hand on his shoulder, resisting the urge to pick him up and carry him. *Let him do as much as he can for himself.* The doctor's words rang in her head, but it was hard, so hard, to watch him struggle.

She settled Jamie at the kitchen table with milk and a banana and then returned to her guest.

Adam greeted her with a question in his eyes. "Do you always keep your son away from people, or is it just me?"

She fidgeted with her glass, disconcerted by his blunt attack. Well, she could be blunt, too. "Jamie's had enough of people staring at him and pitying him."

"I wasn't…" He stopped, and she sensed an emotion she didn't understand working behind the pleasant face he presented to the world.

"Sorry," he said finally. "I guess I overreacted the first time I saw him. I promise, it won't happen again. He has nothing to fear from me."

That was an odd way of expressing it, and again she had the sense of something behind the words.

But there was no time to speculate on it now.

The sound of a car had her stomach twisting in knots again. That would be Emily Warden, bringing Grandpa back from his lunch.

She looked at Adam and saw the same apprehension in his eyes that must be in hers. Ready or not, it was time to do this.

Grandpa's face was already red with anger when he came through the door, no doubt because he'd seen the strange car sitting in front. She steeled herself for the inevitable explosion.

It didn't come. Somehow, Grandpa managed to hold his voice down to a muted roar. "What is he doing here?"

He indicated Adam with a jerk of his head, focusing his glare on her.

"He's here because I invited him." Her voice didn't wobble, thank goodness, as she drew the battle line.

This was actually the first time she'd challenged her grandfather on anything since she'd moved back, but she had to do this. It was the only door out of this trap they were in.

"I told you before. He's nothing to do with us."

"Grandpa, that's not the truth, and you know it. I found this." She held out the watch. It lay on her palm, and her grandfather looked at it as if it were a snake about to strike.

"Where did you get that?"

"In Grandma's trunk." A smile trembled on her lips at the memory of her grandmother. "She never did like to throw anything away. Remember?"

"'Course I remember." His eyes were suspiciously bright. "Woman saved everything. Never listened to me a day in her life. Feisty."

"She had to be, living with you all those years." It was the sort of thing she used to be able to say to him, gone in the aftermath of the quarrel, but it came to her lips now. "Look at the watch, Grandpa. 'To E.B. from Mama and Daddy. 1942.'"

He was shaking his head when Adam held out his own watch.

"I have one, too. The family still gives them as an eighteenth-birthday gift."

Grandpa stared at it for a moment. Then he stumped over to his rocking chair and sat down heavily, the red color slowly fading out of his face, leaving it pale and set.

"All right, all right. Since you're bound and determined to have it out, I was born Edward Bodine. But I haven't been that man in years, and I don't reckon to start now."

The capitulation left her weak in the knees, and she sat down on the sofa, not sure what would come next.

Grandpa stared at Adam, as if seeking some resemblance. "Your grandfather was my little brother. He still alive?"

"No, sir. He died ten years ago of a stroke. Miz Callie's still going strong, though. He married Callie McFarland. You remember her?"

"Little Callie." Her grandfather seemed to look back through the years, and for the first time she saw some softening in his expression. "'Course I remember her. Lived near us on the island, always in and out of the house. So she and Richmond got hitched."

Adam came cautiously to take a seat next to her, apparently feeling he wasn't going to get thrown out at the moment. "Richmond and Callie had three boys. My father is the oldest."

"And you'd be his oldest boy, I s'pose."

Adam blinked. "How did you know that?"

"Oldest sons have that look of responsibility on them." His face tightened a little. "I did. You in the service?"

"Coast Guard. Lieutenant. I'm running a patrol boat out of Coast Guard Base Charleston right now."

So she'd been right about the military look of him. Despite that easygoing smile, he was probably one who could take command when he needed to.

"Family tradition." Grandpa's lips twisted. "Your great-granddaddy would be right proud of you. He never was of me. Called me a coward, said I was a disgrace to the family name. So I figured I didn't need to use it any more."

The bitterness that laced his voice appalled her. How could he still carry so much anger toward someone who was long dead?

She glanced at Adam, to see that he looked taken aback as well.

"It's been a long time, Grandpa." She said the words softly. "Adam and his people didn't have anything to do with the quarrel you had with your father."

"They're his kin," he flared.

"And yours," Adam said. "Miz Callie is the one who was determined to find out what happened to you. She remembers so much about that last summer on the island—about how you took her and Richmond fishing and shrimping, how patient you were with them."

His face eased a little. "They were good kids, I'll say that. Always listened."

"You had some friends there, too. Boys you hung around with in the summer, Miz Callie says. There's a picture of a bunch of you together."

"Timmy Allen and Phil Yancey, I s'pose. And Benny Adams. I haven't thought of them in years. All dead now, I reckon."

"Not Mr. Adams. My sister talked to him just a few weeks ago, once we found out you were still alive. He said to tell you to come see him."

"Benny always was tough, for all he was the shortest one of the bunch." The hand Grandpa raised to his eyes trembled a little, and he wiped away tears.

Her heart twisted. He hadn't wept since Grandma's death. He was softening toward Adam. If only…

"Why don't y'all come back to Charleston with me?" Adam said. "The family there would surely like to get to know you."

Grandpa shook his head. "What's the point in reliving the past? I don't go where I'm not wanted."

"Please," she murmured, barely aware that it was a prayer. Then, more boldly, she said, "The rest of the family would like to meet you, Grandpa. They didn't have anything to do with the quarrel."

She leaned toward him, intent on making him agree to this. Didn't he see? It was a chance for Jamie. Once they got to Charleston, anything could happen. There were specialists there, even a medical university. The family might feel obligated to help.

If not, well, she could talk to a lawyer, even, to see if Grandpa was entitled to some part of his father's estate.

"Miz Callie's going to be disappointed in me if I come back without you," Adam said. "She has her heart set on seeing you again. She's always believed in you."

Grandpa weakened a little; she could see it in his eyes, even though he was still shaking his head.

"Are we goin' someplace, Grandpa?" Jamie, drawn by their voices, poked his head in from the kitchen. "I want to go someplace."

"We might go to Charleston, sugar," she said. That was playing dirty, involving Jamie, but at this point she'd do whatever it took. "You could see the beach. Wouldn't that be great?"

"I want to go." He hurried across the room as fast as his braces would allow, fetching up against his grandfather's knees. "Please, let's go. I want to see the beach."

Grandpa stroked Jamie's silky hair, his hand not quite steady. "Well, I guess maybe there's no harm in going to see the place." He looked at Adam then, "I'm not saying I'll go back to being part of the family, mind, so don't you go getting any ideas. But I guess we can go for a visit, seein' it means so much to the boy."

Cathy exhaled slowly, afraid even to move for fear he'd change his mind. But he wouldn't do that, not once he'd told Jamie.

Her gaze met Adam's, and she smiled. They'd done it.

Chapter Three

Adam shot upright in bed, his heart thudding, wet with perspiration. Disoriented for a moment, until he remembered that he was spending the night at the Hawkins place so they could make an early start in the morning.

Checking his watch, he let the routine movement calm him. Two in the morning. Definitely too early to get up, but his heart still pounded and his nerves jumped, demanding that he move.

It had been the dream. Fragments of it this time, not the whole, inevitable sequence of events he sometimes replayed for himself. In this one, he'd seen the smugglers' boat, black and shining in the sunlight that dazzled his eyes. He'd seen his hands, the right hand clutching his weapon at the ready, heard himself give the command to fire the warning shot.

Then the boat swamping, people tumbling into

the water, reaching for the boy, seeing the look of silent suffering, the mother's anguish as she held him. The blood.

He must have jerked himself awake at that point, overwhelmed with guilt. The guilt was always there, but kept constantly under control. Only his dreams loosed it, like a beast ready to devour him.

Running both hands through his damp hair, he clutched the back of his neck. Hot in here—maybe that was what had triggered the dream. It had been hot that day, too, but cooler once the patrol boat was out on the ocean.

A breath of jasmine-scented air touched her face. No use trying to go back to bed right away. He'd go to the kitchen, get a drink, maybe walk around a little until his nerves settled.

He padded silently down the stairs, reminding himself that the house's three occupants slept behind the doors on the first floor. And thinking of them made him realize exactly why he'd dreamed tonight. It wasn't the heat or the strange bed.

It was Cathy and Jamie. That first glimpse of the boy had done it. He'd seen Cathy bending over her son protectively, seen the look of patient suffering in the boy's eyes, and he'd been right back there on the water off the Florida Keys.

Reaching the kitchen, he drew a glass of water from the tap. Tepid, but he drained it anyway in a long, thirsty gulp. He set the glass on the counter.

Its click was followed by another sound—a creaking board. He turned.

Cathy stood in the doorway. Barefoot like him, she wore a striped robe that fell to her knees. Her hair was pulled back in a braid. Even in the dim light, he could see the question in her eyes.

She crossed to him quietly. "Is something wrong?"

"Just couldn't sleep." He wasn't going to tell her why—not now, not ever, even though it might help to explain his initial reaction to Jamie.

"I don't wonder, with this heat. I'm sure you're used to air-conditioning." She moved to the refrigerator and got out a pitcher of water, picked up his glass and poured. "Have this. At least it's cold."

"Thanks." He took the glass she offered. It was frosty against his palm. "You're not sleeping, either."

She made an indeterminate little gesture with her hand. "Fretting about whether I've forgotten something, I guess. Or whether anything will go wrong."

"I'm not surprised. The arrangements for this trip have been as complicated as planning a NATO summit."

That brought a smile to her face. "You're right about that. I thought a dozen times in the past couple of days that Grandpa would cancel the whole visit."

"Luckily we had our secret weapon."

At her look of incomprehension, he grinned. "Jamie. That boy could charm the birds from the trees. He reminds me of my brother, Cole. Cole can talk anybody into most anything."

She tilted her head to one side, looking at him. "Is Cole like you?"

"In looks, you mean? He's not as big as I am—more wiry, I guess you'd say. Not in temperament, either. I'm like my daddy, slow and solid. Maybe a little bit boring. Cole, he's like quicksilver, gets mad fast, gets over it fast. I guess that's why he's flying a jet instead of running a patrol boat like me."

"I don't think you're boring," she said. "And it's surely a good thing you're patient, or planning this trip with my grandfather would have driven you crazy."

"It's okay. He has to have mixed feelings about going back after all this time." He paused, wondering if she had any more insight than he did. She and her grandfather didn't seem all that close. "Do you have any idea why he's refusing to go to the beach house? My grandmother just assumed he'd want to stay there. I think she's a little hurt that y'all are going to my mama and daddy's in Mount Pleasant instead."

She ran a hand over her hair, smoothing it back into the loose single braid, maybe buying time. "He hasn't talked to me about it, but I'm guessing he won't go there because that's where he had the big breach with his father. Too many bad memories, maybe."

He considered that. "Bound to be some good ones, too, but…" He let that trail off, inviting her to finish the thought.

"He hasn't forgiven his father." She shook her head, the braid swinging. "The poor man's been dead for half a century, I s'pose, but Grandpa can't forgive him. He's not good at forgiving."

Something in her tone alerted him. "It sounds as if you have some personal experience with that."

She didn't speak for a moment—long enough for him to wish he hadn't pried. This trip was going to be difficult enough without having her mad at him the whole time.

She let out her breath in a little sigh. "I know better than anyone." She spread her hands slightly. "You've seen how he is with me. You probably wouldn't believe that we were as close as could be once."

"What happened?" he asked softly, just to keep her talking.

She stared blankly toward the window where a small patch of moonlight showed, but he didn't think she was seeing that.

"I let him down," she said finally. "He had his heart set on my going to college. He and Grandma saved every penny they could to make that happen.

And then I had to lose my head over a guy. Quit college, get married. Break my grandma's heart, to hear Grandpa tell it."

If it had been daylight, she probably never would have said a word of that. The dark, silent kitchen seemed to encourage confidences.

"What you did was only what thousands of other kids probably do every year. It's not so bad."

"It was to Grandpa. He said if I persisted in doing something so foolish, he'd wash his hands of me."

"But you're here now." What had happened to the man? Where did Jamie fit into the story?

"After Jamie was born, my husband left. I worked, but Jamie needed so much care—well, eventually we needed a place to live. Grandpa needed someone to look out for him." She shrugged. "It worked out all right eventually. But I wouldn't count on him forgiving anytime soon."

Her voice had hardened, and she'd warned him off the private, obviously painful past. No matter. She was coming to Charleston, and he'd have time to hear the rest of the story.

"I'm pinning all my hopes on Miz Callie," he said lightly. "This is her heart's desire, and I imagine she can be just as stubborn as your grandfather."

Cathy seemed to shake off the remnants of the past. "Let's hope so, for all our sakes."

Leaning against the counter, he studied her face,

pale and perfect as a black-and-white drawing in the dim light. "There's something I've been wondering about. I know why I'm going to all this trouble to bring Ned back to his family. Why are you?"

She looked startled and defensive, taking a step back. "I...I want what's best for my grandfather, that's all."

Was it? He wasn't so sure. He had a sense that there was more to Cathy's desire to get her family to Charleston than he'd heard.

He'd be patient. He didn't have to know all the answers tonight.

But he would know them, eventually.

"We're going over the Ravenel Bridge now." Adam's voice was cheerful, as it had been for this endless trip.

Jamie, who'd slept in the car, was nearly as energetic as Adam. Her grandfather had slept off and on. Or maybe he'd just been closing his eyes against the once-familiar sights.

As for her—well, she was just plain exhausted. All the emotional stress and the hard work of the past few days seemed to have landed on her once she was sitting still. It was all she could do to keep her eyes open.

Jamie leaned forward eagerly in his booster seat, hanging on Adam's every word. "Is that the ocean down there under the bridge?"

"That's the Cooper River." Adam didn't let a trace of amusement into his voice. "Look at all the boats."

Jamie pressed his face against the window, peering down. "Wow. I wish I could go on a boat."

"Don't talk foolish. You don't need to go on any boats." Grandpa's voice was sharp, startling her.

Jamie's eyes filled with tears at the unexpected rebuke. She patted him, biting her tongue to keep from snapping back at her grandfather. They were all tired. Now was not the time to talk about it.

"We'll see," she said quietly. "Look, we're coming down off the bridge."

"This is Mount Pleasant," Adam said. "It's where I grew up. You're going to sleep in the house where I lived when I was your age."

"I am?" Jamie clearly found that idea exciting. "Are your toys there?"

"Jamie," she said, a warning note in her voice.

"That's okay." Adam's gaze met hers in the rearview mirror. "Tell you what, Jamie. If my mama didn't think to get some of my old toys out of the attic, you and I will go up there tomorrow and find some for you."

Uneasiness edged along her skin. She didn't want Adam doing anything for her son out of pity. Maybe that was irrational, but that was how she felt about it. And she certainly didn't want Jamie to start relying on him. Who knew how long Adam would be a part of their lives?

She should talk to Adam about it. Just explain her feelings calmly and rationally. He'd understand.

But no more private talks alone in dark kitchens. Her cheeks flamed at the memory. What had possessed her to tell him anything about her past?

At least she'd had the sense to keep it brief. She'd make sure he wouldn't be hearing any more. And maybe she'd best be on guard that she didn't start relying on him, either.

She was here for just one reason—to grasp any opportunity that would help Jamie. Nothing else mattered. She summoned up the image of Jamie walking. *Think about that, nothing else.*

Adam turned onto a narrow residential street that seemed to jog right and left without rhyme or reason. The antebellum-style houses were so close together that the neighborhood felt claustrophobic to her. It was a far cry from their isolated farmhouse.

Adam pulled up in front of a graceful brick home, its small front garden filled with flowers.

"Home," Adam announced. "Let's go meet the family."

With a wordless prayer, Cathy reached out to unbuckle Jamie's seat belt. This was what she'd wanted. Now she had to face it.

Adam was there suddenly, lifting Jamie out of

the car. "There you go, buddy. Let's go see if my mama got out any toys for you."

Cathy took her grandfather's arm. To her surprise, he didn't pull away. Together, they walked up the brick path to the house and the people who stood outside, waiting for them.

The next few minutes passed in a flurry of introductions. Adam's father, Ashton, was an older version of Adam, with chestnut hair touched with white at the temples and calm, judicious eyes that seemed to take her measure. His mother was casually elegant, so perfectly coiffed and clad that Cathy felt instantly disheveled and dowdy next to her.

Then a pair of warm arms encircled her as the third member of the welcoming party grabbed her in an unexpected hug.

"I'm Georgia, Adam's sister. Welcome, Cathy. We're so glad you're here."

Nobody could doubt the sincerity of Georgia's greeting, and the cold ball of uncertainty in Cathy began to thaw. "Thank you." She drew Jamie close to her. "This is my son, Jamie."

Georgia knelt, dark curls swinging around her face. "Hey, there, Cousin Jamie. It's so nice to meet you."

Jamie seemed struck dumb by the attention. Then he looked up at Cathy. "Is she really my cousin?" he whispered.

Georgia chuckled. "Sugar, it's too complicated to be anything else."

Cathy reminded herself that they weren't really cousins of hers at all, but if they were willing to see the relationship that way, she wouldn't argue.

Georgia's mother elbowed her aside and held out her hand to Jamie. "Why don't you come with me, Sugar, and we'll see if we can find some toys for you?"

Jamie looked up at her for permission. She fought back the urge to keep him close. "Go along, but don't forget your manners."

"Yes, ma'am." He took Georgia's mother's hand tentatively.

Georgia grinned. "Mama loves having a child around to fuss over. Now, you come along, and Daddy and I will show you to your rooms. You just feel free to rest if you want. If I know my brother, he probably got you up at the crack of dawn to drive here."

"Something like that." She glanced at Grandpa and saw the tiredness and tension in his drawn face. "Maybe a little lie-down would be good."

Georgia nodded, understanding in her eyes. "Come along, then, and we'll get you settled. Adam can bring in your bags before he heads on home."

She turned toward Adam, not that she hadn't been aware every minute of exactly where he was, standing quietly behind her.

"I guess we should say thank you and goodbye, then." She held out her hand, because if he followed his sister's example and hugged her, it might weaken her resolve to keep him at arm's length.

He took her hand in both of his, closing them warmly around hers, and she felt that warmth spreading through her. "Don't be so eager to get rid of me."

"I'm not." Her cheeks warmed. "I just thought you... Well, you probably have things to do besides babysit us."

"No chance. I'll be back later with Miz Callie." His fingers tightened on hers, and his voice lowered. "Relax, Cathy. You have family now."

That hit her right in the heart. She wanted to believe that, but could she?

By the time supper was over, Cathy had hit a wall of exhaustion. Too little sleep and too much worry combined to rob her of even the ability to chat.

Fortunately nobody seemed to expect much of her at the moment. Adam had returned with his grandmother, and just now Miz Callie, as they all called her, sat next to Grandpa, talking away a mile a minute. To her relief, Grandpa looked more relaxed than she'd seen him in days. She'd been half-afraid he'd explode at these new relatives and ruin whatever chance they had.

Jamie sat on the floor of the family room, playing

a game of Chutes and Ladders with Georgia. Georgia was apparently about to become the stepmother of an eight-year-old, and she'd said she'd learned to love children's games again.

Adam had laughed at that, telling her she'd never stopped, and Georgia gibed back at him. For a moment, Cathy had thought they were on the verge of argument, but apparently this sort of good-natured teasing went on all the time between them.

Miz Callie had announced that they were giving them a little time before inflicting the rest of the family on them. Cathy could only feel grateful for that respite.

As it was, the talk, even the kindness of their welcome, was a bit overwhelming. Could anyone really be as warm to a bunch of unknown relatives as the Bodines seemed to be?

Feeling as if she'd fall asleep if she sat in the comfortable chair any longer, she rose. A cabinet against the wall held a dozen or more framed photographs, and she forced her fogged mind to focus on them.

"Admiring my mother's gallery?" Adam's voice came, soft at her shoulder, and her skin prickled in awareness at his nearness.

"This is you," she said, pointing to a solemn young Adam in cap and gown.

"The self-important high-school graduation photo," he said. "I wish she'd get rid of that."

"This looks more like you." She touched the silver-framed snapshot of Adam in Coast Guard blues, leaning against a boat of some sort.

"That's the patrol boat I manned out of Miami for a while."

Some tension entered his voice when he said that, and she looked up at his face, wondering what caused it. But he was moving on, identifying people in other photos. The names blurred in her mind, but…

"A lot of people in uniform," she commented.

"That tends to be a Bodine tradition," he said. "Mostly Coast Guard, like my grandfather. Miz Callie always says that Bodines are never happy too far from the sea."

"My grandfather must be the exception, then. He settled inland, and never seemed to want to go anywhere else."

Half-afraid that her grandfather might hear her speaking of him, she glanced his way, but he seemed engrossed in something Adam's father was saying.

"Let's step out into the garden for a minute." Adam took her arm. "You look as if you can use some fresh air."

Before she could protest, he was guiding her out the French doors onto a flagstone patio. At its edge was a rustic bench, and he led her to a seat in the shadow formed by a live oak draped with Spanish moss, silver in the dim light.

"You've been as tense as a cat in a roomful of rockers all evening. What's wrong?" he asked.

"Just tired, I guess." That was true, but it wasn't all of it.

Adam surveyed her face, his eyes serious, maybe even caring. "It's just been a few days, but I already know you better than that. What are you fretting about?"

This was just what she'd wanted to avoid—being alone with him in the quiet evening, feeling as if she could tell him anything.

"Worried that Grandpa will lose his temper, for one thing. I'd hate for him to alienate everyone before they even get to know him."

Hate for him to ruin Jamie's chance to benefit from being a part of the Bodine family. That was the truth, but she wasn't going to admit that to Adam, no matter how sympathetic she found him.

"They're not going to take offense." He clasped her hand in his. "They know the whole story. They just want to be family again, that's all. If he doesn't…"

Tears pricked at her eyes. "I pushed him into this. If it doesn't work out, I'm to blame."

"Seems to me you take entirely too much

blame on yourself." He brushed a strand of hair back from her cheek, and his fingers left a trail of awareness in their wake.

She looked up at him, startled, to find his face very close. "Adam, I…" She lost whatever she'd been going to say. All she could think about was how near he was.

She saw the same recognition in his eyes—a little startled, a little wary. And then the wariness vanished and his lips found hers.

For an instant the world narrowed to the still garden and the touch of Adam's lips. Then reality flooded in and she jerked back, cheeks flaming. She shot to her feet. He rose, too, holding out one hand to her. He seemed about to speak.

She didn't want to hear it, no matter what it was.

"Good night, Adam." She fled into the house before she could make any more of a fool of herself.

Chapter Four

"So when is that old patrol boat going to be replaced with something more up-to-date?"

Adam turned, grinning, at the sound of his cousin Hugh's voice. "Don't talk that way about the best little boat in the southeast." He patted the shining trim. "She might get her feelings hurt."

"You and your boats." Hugh leaned an elbow against the dock railing. "I knew I'd find you here. Anyone would think she was a pretty lady instead of an old tub."

"Don't say that. She might hear you. And not that I don't enjoy exchanging insults with you, but what are you doing down here? The Maritime Law Enforcement Academy having a day off?"

"I don't teach all the time, y'know."

"Tell the truth. You don't want to be teaching at all." He knew only too well that Hugh had loved his work as a boarding officer, leading the crew that boarded suspicious vessels, that he itched to be back on duty. "What do the docs say?"

"Same old, same old," Hugh said gloomily, patting his bad leg. "They don't want me in charge of a boarding crew until I'm a hundred percent."

The injury had hurt Hugh's pride as well as his leg, Adam suspected. He hated the fact that smugglers had gotten the upper hand of him, even for a moment.

"What do doctors know? Anyway, you brought in the bad guys, even with a bullet in your leg."

Hugh shrugged. "I want to get back out there. We've seen an uptick in smuggling operations. I'd be more use out there than standing in front of a chalkboard."

"It'll come." He felt almost ashamed of his healthy state. "Don't push it."

"Well, you be careful when you're out there, y'heah? It's not all just Sunday sailors running out of fuel these days." Hugh straightened, pressing his hands back against the railing.

"I always am." A trail of unease went through him as he said the words. If he'd been as careful as he claimed, he wouldn't have injured a child.

And if he'd been as careful as he should be, he wouldn't have kissed Cathy last night.

Hugh reached out to thump the side of the boat. "So, speaking of pretty ladies, what is our new stepcousin like? When are the rest of us going to get a look at her?"

Adam's uneasiness increased. "That's up to Miz Callie. She seemed to think we might be a little overwhelming all at once."

"The Bodines? Overwhelming?" Hugh exhibited mock surprise. "Never. So I suppose you're Miz Callie's hero now, finding our missing uncle and all."

"I don't feel like much of a hero."

The concerns he had about the whole situation pushed at him. He hadn't talked to anyone about it, but he could talk to Hugh. Hugh's law-enforcement background gave him a shrewd eye for anything that might cause trouble.

"So what is it?" Hugh asked, confirming his thoughts. "Something's bothering you about them. Is it Uncle Ned or the granddaughter?"

"Both." He frowned, trying to frame his words. "From what I can tell, Ned...or Hawkins, as I guess he prefers, has been nursing a grudge against the family all these years."

Hugh pursed his lips in a silent whistle. "I knew he was on the outs with his father, but that's more than fifty years ago. How can he blame the rest of us?"

"I'm not saying it's rational. And he did agree to come, so maybe..." He let that thought die off.

"Has Miz Callie talked to him at all about this

memorial she has planned? I mean, he's not dead yet, so he might think a memorial is a tad premature. What if he doesn't want a nature preserve named after him?"

"You've got me. Apparently Ned never talks about his war years, so he may not like the idea of being reminded. I just hope this whole thing hasn't set Miz Callie up for disappointment. I wouldn't want her to get hurt."

"If it doesn't go the way she hopes, well… It's not like she's going to blame you for that."

"I feel responsible. I'm the one who tracked him down."

"Because she wanted you to." Hugh was nothing if not practical. "You don't always have to be the responsible one, y'know."

He grinned in response to the familiar gibe, but it didn't make him feel any better. It was a family joke only because it was true. He was the responsible one, always the one the others depended on.

Hugh tilted his head back toward the sun and pulled on the brim of his Coast Guard ball cap. "So I hear tell from Georgia something's wrong with the little boy. What's the story?"

"I wish I knew." Frustration sounded in the words. "I spent the better part of four days with them, and Cathy still keeps me at arm's length. I get the impression it's something he was born with, though. Wrenches my heart, seeing him lift those heavy braces."

She hadn't kept her distance last night, the little voice in his head reminded him. *Last night you were considerably closer than that, and you shouldn't have been.*

"She didn't talk to you at all about the kid?" Hugh's voice made it clear he'd have asked.

"She's overprotective. Secretive, I guess you'd say." And he was attracted to her, despite not being sure he trusted her.

Hugh leaned against the rail, frowning. "I suppose there's no doubt he really is Ned Bodine, is there?"

"Oh, he's Ned, all right. I matched up the photos, and he has the watch his parents gave him."

Hugh gave a quick glance at his own watch. "Well, even granting he's kin, we still don't know anything about him. Or this stepgranddaughter of his. It might be just as well to be a little cautious."

"Can you picture Miz Callie being cautious, now that she's found Granddad's brother after all these years?" Exasperation leaked into his voice.

"You've got a point there." Hugh's frown deepened. "So, it sounds like you'd best be keeping a close eye on them."

"Me? Why me?" He'd just been thinking it might be wise to keep his distance from Cathy for a bit.

"You're the one they know. If they're going to let anything slip, it'll be to you. Besides—" Hugh clapped him on the shoulder "—you're Miz Callie's hero, remember?"

Adam's jaw tightened. Hugh was joking, that was all. He couldn't imagine how little Adam felt like a hero these days.

Her grandfather had been feeling the effects of the trip, growing increasingly irritable as the morning wore on. When he'd finally agreed to take a nap after lunch, Cathy could only feel relieved. She came slowly back downstairs after settling him, running her hand on the polished stair railing. Adam's parents' house didn't scream money, but it had an atmosphere of quiet elegance that didn't come cheap.

For a moment she felt a hot flush of shame at putting a mental price tag on the home of her hosts. Adam would look at her in contempt if he knew.

But how could she help drawing a comparison between this place and the rundown farmhouse they called home? As for Adam—well, he would never know what she was thinking. And she knew perfectly well that his name and his face were only coloring her thoughts because of that kiss.

What had possessed him? Or her, for that matter? She hadn't exactly been fighting him off.

She'd say that was because she'd been taken so

much by surprise, but lying to herself was a bad idea. She'd been surprised, all right. She'd also been overwhelmed with need and longing. Some deep, aching emptiness inside her had been brought to life by the touch of his lips.

Forget it, she ordered herself firmly. It meant nothing. She would make it mean nothing. Adam had given in to a momentary impulse.

She went in search of Jamie, who'd been settled in the family room with a book when she went upstairs. Now he was in the garden, sitting on a rug with some toys while Miz Callie sat in a lawn chair, watching him.

Cathy took a deep breath, her hand on the door. No two ways about it, Miz Callie intimidated her. Miz Callie might be a tiny, slight elderly woman, but she packed a lot of character in that wise face. Cathy could understand why Adam, indeed the whole family, seemed to have such respect for her.

Stiffening her backbone, Cathy went out into the garden, trying not to look in the direction of that bench where Adam had kissed her.

"Cathy." Miz Callie looked up with a welcoming smile. "Please, come sit with me. We need to get better acquainted." She patted the chair that had been placed next to her.

Pinning a smile to her face, Cathy obediently sat. "I hope Jamie isn't being troublesome."

"Goodness, no. He's been as good as gold, sitting there playing with those little wooden trains Delia found for him."

"That was nice of her." She could see that Jamie was totally preoccupied with the brightly colored trains.

"They were Adam's when he was a boy," Miz Callie said. "I remember when an addition to his train set was the perfect Christmas or birthday present for him. When he was about Jamie's age, that would have been."

She didn't want to talk about Adam, because just hearing his name made her cheeks grow hot, and she feared Miz Callie would notice something. Still, she ought to keep Miz Callie talking about the family. Anything she learned might be of help. She firmly suppressed the qualms she felt. This was for Jamie.

"Such a sweet boy." Miz Callie was looking at Jamie. "You must be proud of him."

That took her so much by surprise that it took her a moment to react. "Yes, I am. You'd be surprised at the number of people who just want to pity him. Or me."

"I've never been overly impressed with the wisdom of most people," Miz Callie said drily.

That surprised a laugh out of her. She was beginning to see what it was about Miz Callie that had her children and grandchildren so devoted to her.

"They only see his disability," Cathy said. "But he's like any child, otherwise. A little naughty sometimes. Funny. Loving." There was suddenly a lump in her throat.

Miz Callie nodded. "They can all be naughty, can't they? I remember some of the things my grandkids got into. Land, what one of them didn't think of, the others did."

"They're all close in age, Adam told me."

Miz Callie nodded, a smile on her face that seemed to indicate she was looking back on those years when they were small. "Cole, that's Adam's brother, he was the worst for leading them into mischief."

"Let me guess. It was Adam who led them back out again."

"You're very perceptive. That's exactly right. How did you guess?"

She shrugged, a little uncomfortable at having the conversation turned to the person she didn't want to think about right now. "He strikes me as being very responsible, that's all."

"He's our rock, is Adam. It's interesting that you saw that so quickly."

She wouldn't let herself be led down the pathway of talking about Adam. "I take it you were able to spend a lot of time with your grandkids, living here in the Charleston area."

"It's been a blessing having them so close most

of the time. In the summers, they'd always come out to the island house to spend time with their grandfather and me. Those were the best times."

"What did you do with them? It seems like a lot, all those kids."

"It was a joy," Miz Callie said. "And really, they did just what our kids had done as children. And what Richmond and I had done, too, summers on the island."

Her image of the Bodine clan was growing, Cathy realized. Not an image of great wealth, no, but of a family that was comfortably off in a way that her family had never been.

What would a lawyer say, if she consulted one? Would Grandpa be entitled to anything from the family? It might depend...

"Jamie's disability," Miz Callie said gently. "I take it that's something he was born with?"

The question was asked so tenderly that Cathy couldn't muster her usual offended response. Besides, if she wanted their help, it would come at the cost of her privacy.

"He was born with spina bifida." She kept her voice even. "There were some other abnormalities of his hips, as well."

Miz Callie made a small sound of distress. "He's had surgery, has he?"

"Several times." She had to swallow before she could keep going, remembering how painful those times had been. And how brave Jamie was. "He's in good shape now, in comparison. The last specialist he saw seemed to think one more surgery might be all it takes for him to walk."

"That's good news, surely." Miz Callie gave her a cautious sideways glance. "The father isn't a part of his life?"

"He walked out when Jamie was a few weeks old." She hated the sound of the bitterness in her voice. "Grandpa said he wasn't the type to hang around, and he was right."

"Not a thing I'd be glad to be right about," Miz Callie observed.

It took a moment for that to register. But Miz Callie had hit the nail on the head. Grandpa had been perversely pleased to be proved right. She didn't like thinking that.

"You have to understand," she said hurriedly. "I let him and my grandmother down when I quit school to marry. My education was their dream."

"It's always dangerous to have specific dreams for your children and grandchildren. Life so often takes them in another direction. I find I have to count on the good Lord to get them to the place where they belong."

Cathy found she was looking at Jamie, tracing the line of his cheeks, the feathery hair around his ears. "It's hard not to want specific things for our children."

"Hard, land, yes. We always want to be in control, don't we? I keep reminding myself that God knows better than I do what's good for them."

"I'm afraid I haven't been able to do that." Her prayers were more in the nature of storming Heaven for answers.

"Ah, well. You've had your hands full with your son and your grandfather." A faint line deepened between Miz Callie's brows. "Is Ned always so… well, closed in?"

"I'm afraid so. At least, since Grandma died. She was the one person who could get through to him. She'd stir him up, get him interested in life."

"It's a blessing he had her, then." Miz Callie's eyes filled with tears. "I remember him as a teenager, before all the trouble with his papa. He was older than us, of course, but always so kind. Interested in what we were doing, and endlessly patient. That last summer at the island…" She let the words die out.

Cathy was seized by the same desire Adam must feel—the need to protect her from hurt. "Miz Callie, I don't think he can go back to being the person you remember."

"Gracious, child, I know that." Miz Callie grasped her hand in a surprisingly firm grip. "We can't go back, any of us. We just have to move forward and make the most of each day. I'm so glad to see him again after all this time. I'd hoped he'd want to come out to the island house, but he seems set against it."

Going to the island was such a small thing, but once Grandpa made up his mind, changing it was no easy matter. "Maybe he'll reconsider," she said, knowing her voice didn't extend much hope.

"We won't worry about it," Miz Callie said. "But you and Jamie should come out. Jamie would love the beach, I know. You can't come all this way without paying your respects to the ocean."

"I'd like that, but…" But she didn't want to make her grandfather angry. She'd been on edge since this trip started, hoping to keep him from flying off the handle and ruining everything.

"We'll see." Miz Callie patted her hand and released it. "If you decide to come, just let Adam know. He can drive you out."

Alarm bells went off in her mind. Why had Miz Callie said that Adam would do it? There were certainly plenty of other people around who could take her.

Did Miz Callie suspect that there was something between her and Adam? She couldn't, Cathy told herself firmly. There was nothing to suspect.

So why couldn't she rid herself of this uneasiness?

Cathy had found it necessary to talk fast in order to convince Delia, Adam's mother, to let her help with supper that night. She couldn't do nothing but take care of Grandpa and Jamie. It didn't feel right not to pitch in.

Delia had finally agreed, and the hour they'd spent together in the kitchen had made her feel somewhat easier in the woman's presence. But she was still a bit taken aback by Delia's casual elegance. The woman could make a pair of slacks and a summer shirt look like something from the pages of a fashion magazine.

Georgia, Adam's sister, was considerably less intimidating. Tonight she'd brought her fiancé and soon-to-be stepdaughter with her to dinner. Apparently this was part of Miz Callie's plan to introduce them gradually to the rest of the family.

"Oh, no. I've hit a chute again." Eight-year-old Lindsay's voice floated over those of the adults, who now lingered at the table over coffee and pecan pie.

Lindsay had decided that she and Jamie should play a board game instead of listen to adult talk, and she'd led Jamie off to a corner of the family room.

Cathy glanced that way. So far it seemed to be going well, but she kept an ear tuned to their voices, ready to intervene if necessary. Jamie so seldom had other children to play with that it was hard to predict how he'd react.

She was carefully avoiding looking at the person

who sat opposite her at the table. Adam had come in when they were nearly ready to sit down to eat. If Delia had been surprised at his appearance, she'd quickly masked it, giving him a kiss on the cheek and setting another place at the table.

She was fine as long as she wasn't alone with him, Cathy assured herself. Given a little more time, the memory of that kiss would fade, and they could be alone without having it the chief topic on their minds. She didn't want an apology. She didn't want to discuss it. She just wanted to forget.

"Business picking up, Matt?" Adam's big hand dwarfed the delicate china cup he held as he asked the question.

"Some," Matt Harper said. His attention never seemed to stray far from Georgia and Lindsay, but for the moment he focused on Adam. "Folks don't seem as intent on suing their neighbors or writing their wills during the summer, for some reason. Now that it's fall, they're ready to get serious again."

So Matt must be an attorney. What would he say if she asked him about anything that might be owed to Grandpa? She couldn't, of course, but she might need someone with legal knowledge to sort this out.

"Y'all know that everyone's invited for supper on Saturday night, don't you?" Delia said. "We want to give our guests a chance to meet everyone."

Delia seemed focused on her hostess duties. How did she really feel about having three previously unknown relatives foisted on her? If she was upset, Cathy had the feeling she'd never betray that fact.

"What do you want me to bring, Mama?" Georgia asked. "Is a hot appetizer all right?"

"Fine, darlin', fine. Whatever you have time to fix." Delia fixed her gaze on her son. "Adam, you're not going to be on duty, are you? Not that I'm not used to having the Coast Guard disrupt my meal plans, but it would be nice to put on a dinner once and have everybody there."

"I'm not on duty, Mama. And if anything comes up, I'll do my best to switch off with someone."

His father set down his coffee cup. "Any fresh reports on smuggling operations?"

"No, sir. They're mighty well organized, it seems."

"And well-armed, from the scuttlebutt I've heard. You be careful out there."

It hadn't occurred to her that Adam's job was dangerous, but that seemed to be the implication.

"No fair." Jamie's voice fluted out, sounding tearful. "You won again."

She glanced toward the children and put down her napkin. Maybe she'd better—

Georgia put a hand on her arm to stop her. "They'll be fine. I guarantee you, he's going to win the next round. Lindsay is very kindhearted."

"You and she make a good team, then," Matt said, capturing her hand, his gaze warming when he looked at her. "Because you're pretty much that way, too."

Cathy studied her empty coffee cup. What would it be like to have someone looking at her that way? But it was highly unlikely that anyone could describe her as warmhearted. She was tough, because she'd had to be.

"Cathy, Miz Callie was telling me what you said about Jamie's birth defects," Delia said. "I hope you don't mind, but it made me think of my sister-in-law. She knows about those kinds of things."

Cathy nodded, feeling at sea. She hadn't expected Miz Callie to keep those facts private, but she hadn't expected news to get around the family that quickly. "Is she a doctor?" she asked.

"As usual, my mama is assuming other people know what she does," Adam said. "Aunt Julia is an inveterate volunteer at a local hospital, and she serves on the board."

"I was explaining it quite well, Adam," Delia said. "Julia knows all the doctors over there, and I'm sure she'd be delighted to set up an appointment for Jamie with a specialist. Only if you want to, of course, but we have some very fine doctors there, and I'm sure Jamie would receive the very best of attention."

For a moment she couldn't speak. Was the thing

she wanted most going to drop into her lap that easily? But no one was offering to do anything more than set up an appointment with a specialist. And she probably couldn't even manage the consultation fee.

"Mama, maybe Cathy is perfectly happy with the doctor she has now," Adam said, apparently picking up on her lack of response. "I know you think Charleston doctors are better than anyone else's, but Cathy may already have a good doctor—"

"The man's a quack," Grandpa said.

"Not that," she said quickly. "He does his best. Maybe a little old-fashioned, is all."

"Nonsense." Her grandfather glared at her. "If you have a chance to have the boy seen by somebody good, don't be stubborn."

He was a fine one to talk about being stubborn, but she wouldn't say so. The Bodines already looked a bit embarrassed at how Grandpa spoke to her, and she wouldn't compound it by arguing.

"I didn't mean," Delia began.

Cathy shook her head quickly. "It was a kind thought. I'd be grateful for anything she can do." And then she'd figure out how she was going to pay for it.

"You can trust Aunt Julia," Georgia said, putting her cup down. "And now, I think we'd better remind Lindsay that tomorrow's a school day."

Matt nodded, with an affectionate glance at

his daughter. "They can continue the game on Saturday."

Cathy stood, starting to pick up dessert plates. Adam's voice cut across the murmurs of goodbyes and last-minute thoughts.

"It'll be light out for another hour, Cathy. Let me take you and Jamie down to the park for a bit."

Her mind flooded with all the reasons why that was impossible. She couldn't say the most pressing one, obviously "I don't think—"

"Do go, Cathy." Delia took the dishes from her hands. "There's not a thing you need to do here, and you really should take Jamie to Alhambra. It's the most delightful little park right here in Mount Pleasant."

She would look like a spoilsport if she refused after that. Would Delia be so eager to send Cathy off with her son if she knew they'd been kissing in the garden? Somehow she doubted it. A penniless single mother with a disabled child was hardly the person she'd want her oldest son involved with.

She glanced at Adam, receiving the distinct impression that he knew exactly what was going through her mind, which was why he'd asked her in front of everyone.

She managed to unclench her jaw. She might be the poor country cousin, but she knew how to respond to an invitation.

"Thank you, Adam. That sounds nice."

Chapter Five

Adam lifted the child-size wheelchair from the trunk when they reached the playground, his heart clenching. Apparently Jamie needed the chair to do anything more ambitious than get around the house.

The last time he'd seen Juan, the boy had been in a wheelchair, too. Adam had raced him down the hospital corridor to the children's playroom, trying to get a smile from the kid.

It had worked, too. Juan had smiled and chattered as he played with a small red plastic fire engine, so happy with the toy that Adam had gone out afterward and bought one for him.

He'd been holding it in his hand when he'd arrived at the boy's hospital room the next day to find the bed empty. Juan and his mother had been sent back to Cuba.

"Wow." Jamie leaned perilously far forward in

the wheelchair. He wasn't looking at the playground equipment, but at the water beyond. "Is that the ocean?"

Adam brought himself firmly back to the present. "Nope, that's not it. But if we got into a boat and followed the water far enough, we'd get to the ocean."

"Can we do that?" Jamie twisted around in the chair to look up at him. "Can we, please?"

"Jamie, you shouldn't ask for things," Cathy said quickly. "Cousin Adam is very busy with his work."

"Not as busy as all that." He pushed the chair into the park. "What do you think, buddy? Should we go on the swings first?"

Distracted, Jamie pulled on the arms of the chair, as if to make it go faster. "Yes, sir. Swings."

He veered the chair off the walk, negotiating the sandy soil that dragged at the wheels. He glanced at Cathy. She was watching her son, her expression compounded, he thought, of pleasure at the boy's happiness and worry, probably that he'd do too much.

Which just served, in turn, to remind him of how little he knew about Jamie's condition. And how irked he was that Cathy had told his grandmother before she'd told him.

That sounded petty, put like that, but he couldn't

help it. She hadn't let him in on something that was obviously the most important thing in her life.

"You hang on, now, Jamie." He settled the boy on the swing seat, feeling a qualm of doubt. Was this something Jamie could manage? But Cathy was smiling. Since she was as protective as a mother bear, he figured she wouldn't be smiling if it wasn't okay.

He pulled the swing back and let go.

"Higher, higher," Jamie chanted. "Higher."

"Okay, here you go." He gave the swing another push and glanced at Cathy. She stood beside him, the breeze off the water tossing fine strands of hair across her forehead.

"You tell me if I'm doing too much," he said quietly.

She nodded, her gaze meeting his for a second and then shifting quickly away. "He should be fine. He loves the playground and doesn't get much chance to go."

"Why's that?" He put the question casually, just wanting to keep the conversation going.

She shrugged. "You've seen how far out in the country we live. We usually go to town about once a week, and I try to stop at the playground there if we have time."

He bit his tongue to keep from asking why she didn't go a bit more often if it brought the boy that much pleasure.

"You're flying like a bird, Jamie," he said instead.

Jamie leaned back in the swing, the wind tossing his hair, a blissful grin on his face. "I'm a bird, Mama. A great big hawk."

"You must be a seagull," she said. "There are more seagulls here."

Jamie straightened. "There's some right there."

For a heart-stopping second, Adam thought he was going to let go of the swing rope to point, but instead Jamie nodded toward the water. "Can we go see them up close?"

"Sure thing." Adam slowed the swing. "We should have brought some bread crumbs. They're so greedy they'd practically sit on your lap if you fed them."

"I'm not sure we want them sitting on our laps." Cathy steadied the chair as he lifted her son into it. Adam's hand brushed hers as he did so, and for a moment he imagined that her skin warmed where he touched.

Pulling his mind firmly away from that speculation, he pushed the chair toward the walk that ran along the water.

"Seagulls," Jamie exclaimed with satisfaction. "Look at them, Mama. Cousin Adam, why aren't they all the same?"

That was a quick observation, it seemed to him. Maybe Jamie was good at noticing things because his disability had forced him into being an onlooker most of the time.

"There are several different types of gulls." He pulled the chair up next to a bench. Sitting down next to Jamie, he leaned close to point them out. "That one is a laughing gull. You can tell because of the black hood on its head."

"Wow." Jamie leaned forward as if he wanted to take off after the gulls and wheel over the water, too. "Why is it called a laughing gull? Does it laugh?"

"Not exactly, but its call sounds like a laugh." He scoured his mind for other gull lore that might interest the child. "Those are herring gulls. See the yellow beaks with the little red spots?"

"Herring gulls," Jamie repeated solemnly, as if committing it to memory.

"That's impressive." Cathy sat down next to him. "I didn't even know there were different types of gulls."

"If you'd grown up here, you would," he said, and then wondered if that had been entirely tactful. If Ned had come back to his family sooner, she might well have grown up here. How different might her life have turned out then? On the other hand, if Ned had come home after the war, he'd probably never have met Cathy's grandmother.

Miz Callie would say there was no use arguing

with the past. Just pick up where you are and move forward. And probably she'd be right.

"Look, Mama. That man is feeding the birds."

Sure enough, an elderly man seated on a bench some ten feet away had taken a paper bag from his pocket. He tossed a handful of bread crumbs in the air. The gulls swooped toward them instantly, squawking and flapping as they fought for each morsel.

Entranced, Jamie wheeled his chair toward them. The man smiled at him and tossed another handful of crumbs. Adam raised a questioning eyebrow at Cathy.

"He's all right," she said, but her fingers twisted together in her lap. "We're supposed to let him do anything he can on his own."

"But it's hard," he said. He'd like to put his hand over those straining fingers, but he suspected that wouldn't be well-received.

"Yes, it is." Her voice was soft, her gaze on her son.

"When are you going to let me take you both to the beach? You know he'd love it."

"I…I don't know. My grandfather just seems a little funny about that, for some reason."

"Just because he doesn't want to go doesn't mean you and Jamie shouldn't see the ocean."

"That's what Miz Callie said. She wants us to come out to the beach house."

"You talked to her about Jamie." The words were out before he could stop them, even knowing they sounded petty.

She turned a startled gaze on him. "What about Jamie?"

"About his disability." He'd gone this far. He may as well say the rest of it. "You don't usually talk about that."

"Your grandmother has a way of getting people to confide in her."

That was true enough. He could testify to that, and probably the rest of his cousins could, too.

"You haven't talked to me about it."

That was a trace of surprise in her face. "I guess it just didn't come up. Besides, most people don't want to hear about other folks' troubles."

"I'm not most people."

She shrugged, and her gaze evaded his. "There's not all that much to tell. Jamie was born with spina bifida. That's a condition where part of the spine can be exposed. Fortunately his wasn't the most severe type, but he's had to have several surgeries."

And her husband had walked away at the prospect of raising a disabled child, so she'd faced those operations alone. That he knew.

"Is that why he needs the braces?"

"Not exactly." She gave him a quick glance that seemed to gauge how interested he really was. "There was an abnormality of his hips, as well."

"And can't that be corrected?" Maybe he was asking too many questions, but he wanted to get everything out in the open.

"The specialists think it may be possible." Something guarded came into her eyes. "But it would take another surgery."

"When is he going to have that?" This was beginning to feel like a game of twenty questions. Why was she so reluctant to confide in him?

"I don't know if…" She let that trail off.

"You don't know if you'll go through with it? Why?" He shot a glance at Jamie. "He deserves every chance he can get, just like any kid does."

Juan had deserved that, too, but he hadn't gotten it.

"You think I don't know that?" Her voice rose; her eyes snapped. "We don't have any insurance. You try convincing a doctor and hospital to undertake complex surgery in that situation, and see how far you get."

She clamped her lips shut, looking as if she regretted having said a word to him.

He couldn't let it go at that. "I didn't realize. But aren't there state programs that fund things like that? Or couldn't you—"

"Do you think I haven't tried every option?" She glared at him, maybe glad to have a target for her anger. "What kind of mother do you think I am?"

"Look, I didn't mean to offend you." Now he did clasp her hand in his. "I just… It took me by surprise, that's all, that you don't have insurance."

"It's not something you people would ever have to worry about."

You people, she'd said, with more than a trace of bitterness in her voice. You people, meaning the Bodine family. Well, true enough. If that had happened to any of them, it would have been covered. Growing up a military dependent, he'd certainly never lacked for medical care.

"I'm sorry," he said. That seemed to cover both his thoughtlessness and his perceived advantages over her.

She pulled her hand away, not looking at him. "It's all right," she muttered. She crossed her arms, hugging them close to her chest. Shutting him out.

Maybe he knew why she wanted to shut him out. Why she'd confided in his grandmother instead of him. That impulsive kiss was getting in the way.

He took a deep breath, hoping he was doing the right thing. "Cathy, about last night. When we kissed," he added, in case there was any doubt. "I'm attracted to you, but I shouldn't have acted on that feeling. I see that now. I…we shouldn't added that into the mix just now. We've got enough to handle as it is. So let's just put that aside for the moment. Okay?"

Keeping her gaze fixed firmly on the horizon, she nodded. "That's probably best."

Okay. He'd cleared the air between them, and that was all he could do.

Cathy was battling with mixed feelings, and she didn't like it. She flipped open the Charleston telephone directory and began looking through the listings for attorneys, trying to push every other consideration to the back of her mind.

The attempt failed. She rested the directory on the shining surface of the writing desk in the study. At least, she supposed the room would be called a study, or a library, maybe, with its shelves of books. A small oval table stood in front of the window, holding a Chinese vase filled with burgundy mums that matched the burgundy shade in the room's Oriental carpet. Elegant, like the woman who'd put them there.

Growing up in a house like this, what had Adam thought of their place, with its faded linoleum, scarred table, and sagging couch. Well, never mind. She could figure that one out.

And there she was, back at Adam again. What was wrong with her? She'd come here with the aim of finding some way this turn of events could help Jamie. Yet the first time she'd had an opportunity to tell Adam about his needs, she'd come off as sulky as a spoiled child. She'd been embarrassed.

No, tell the truth. She'd been humiliated. She pressed her fingers against her temples. She had to do something. She couldn't just let this chance slip away, go back home to the way things had always been. If this was an opportunity to change her son's life for the better, she had to grasp it.

She pulled the phone book toward her again, frowning at the list of names. This was a terrible way to go about finding an attorney, even she knew that. She ought to have a recommendation. And she had to be sure whoever she talked to wasn't a good friend to one or another of the Bodine clan.

Maybe she'd be better off trying to find out how to gain access to her grandfather's father's will. If Grandpa had been mentioned in it, that would be a positive step forward. Maybe…

"Hey, Cathy. What are you looking for?"

Cathy slammed the phone book closed as Georgia came in, looking prettier than the flowers in a cool lime-colored blouse and tan slacks, her brown curls held back by a topaz clip.

"Hey, Georgia. I didn't know you were here. I was just…just wondering where the closest pharmacy is. I might need to refill Grandpa's heart medicine while we're here."

"He's all right, isn't he?" Georgia's eyes clouded with concern.

"He's doing well, but he is eighty-six. He gets

out of breath if he exerts too much, and sometimes he's a little forgetful."

That worried Cathy more than she wanted to let on. As crotchety as Grandpa could be, she couldn't bear to think of life without him.

"Well, the pharmacy we use is right along the main drag out toward Sullivan's Island. I'm sure it would be no trouble to transfer a prescription there." She pulled the phone book over, riffled through the yellow pages, and circled a number. "There you are."

"Thanks." She might have to do that, depending on how long Grandpa wanted to stay. He seemed settled enough, but at any moment he could easily decide he wanted to go home. She might not have much time to do what she'd intended.

"Anyway, I stopped by to see if you and Jamie would like to come with me to a program at Lindsay's school. The children are singing, and she'd be tickled to death to have a few more of her people in the audience."

"Now?" Leaving aside the question of whether Lindsay would consider them "her people," she wasn't sure what Grandpa would think of her going off.

"No hurry, but you don't have to change for this. It's very casual."

"I…" Well, why not? Jamie would enjoy it. "I'll have to check with Grandpa. And see how dirty

Jamie has managed to get. I think they're in the garden."

As it turned out, her grandfather was dozing in a lawn chair while Miz Callie played a board game with Jamie.

"You go right on," she said the minute Georgia filled her in. "I'll be happy to sit here with Ned."

Ten minutes later, they were in Georgia's car. Jamie peered out the window, excited to be going anywhere. He seemed to be thriving on the change of scenery and the excitement of doing something different every day.

"The pharmacy is coming up on the right." Georgia pointed. "So you can see it's not far. And there's a supermarket here on the left."

They passed the string of shops and businesses, and soon the scenery leveled out to flat marshland. The sky seemed enormous here, uninterrupted by the mountains she was so used to seeing.

"It's nice that you were able to get off to go to Lindsay's program." She tried to remember if anyone had said what Georgia did.

"Since I'm my own boss, I didn't hesitate to give myself permission. I do marketing and advertising for a number of small businesses in the area. After Matt and I are married, I want to be at home for Lindsay as much as possible."

So much happiness filled Georgia's voice that a pang of pure envy pierced Cathy. But that was foolishness. She had her son. She didn't have room in her life for anyone else.

"How did you and Matt meet?" She'd make up for that envy by giving the bride-to-be the chance to talk about her groom.

"Well, it's really thanks to your grandfather, in a way." Georgia smiled at her expression. "Honestly. You see, Miz Callie had this plan to donate some land for a nature preserve, and she wanted to name it the Edward Bodine Nature Preserve."

"After my grandfather." She still wasn't used to the fact that that was really Grandpa's name.

"As a memorial, you see, because everyone thought he was dead. She kept it secret, thinking the family would be upset, and she hired Matt to take care of the legalities."

She understood hiring a lawyer. "Adam said you all were afraid she'd be hurt by what she found out."

"Anyway, I came to stay at the beach house with Miz Callie to try and find out what was going on, and there Matt was living right next door, and Miz Callie's cause threw us together. Things sort of happened between us. You know how it is."

Yes, she knew, although her romance hadn't turned out well. "I wish you both all the happiness in the world."

"The three of us," Georgia said. "I love Lindsay as much as if she were my flesh and blood, believe me."

She nodded. She'd seen them together, and the love they shared was apparent. She glanced back at Jamie, wishing she dared hope for that for him. For herself. Her heart seemed to frost over. If Jamie's father hadn't been able to stick with them, how could she expect anyone else to?

"Jamie, look out there. See that mud, where the marsh grass is growing? That's called pluff mud."

"Pluff mud," he repeated, seeming to add that to his store of lowcountry knowledge.

"Across this bridge, and we're on the island. It always feels a little magical to me, crossing onto the island."

"It's beautiful," Cathy said. The island stretched out, low and green, and beyond it she could catch a glimpse of the sea. "Look, Jamie, there's the ocean."

"Where, Mama? I can't see it."

"Bless your heart," Georgia said, "we have time. We'll take a little tour and drive past the beach house. You'll get a good view from there."

Georgia drove past a few shops and restaurants and then turned toward the ocean. "Look there," she pointed, drawing to the side of the road. "That's Miz Callie's house, and there's the ocean."

"Wow." That was rapidly becoming Jamie's

favorite word. "Wow. Mama, it's so big. Did you know it would be that big?"

"I thought it might be." She'd been to the ocean once, when she was in college, but even so, the vastness surprised her all over again. The expanse of sand and water and sky seemed to go on forever.

"We'll come another day and you can play on the sand," Georgia said. "Now we'll drive down past Fort Moultrie, and then we'd best get to the school."

"Fort Moultrie?"

"Its sister fort, Fort Sumter, is more famous, but we're very attached to our own little fort. Sullivan's Island has been defending Charleston since before the Revolution, even." Georgia pulled up opposite the low green mounds, pointing to the cannons that faced out to sea. "Maybe that's why Charleston has such a military tradition. It's always been about the military—Coast Guard, Navy, Air Force."

"Especially the Coast Guard, it seems, for your family," Cathy said. "Adam talked a little about that."

"Yes." Georgia was silent for a moment, staring absently at the flag whipping in the wind over the fort. "Adam's been set on the Coast Guard for his career since he was a kid. He never thought of anything else." There was something in her tone that hinted—well, Cathy wasn't sure what it hinted.

That something was wrong, maybe? Or was she just hypersensitive where Adam was concerned?

"Are you worried about him?" she said finally.

Georgia's forehead wrinkled. "Not worried, exactly. Just sort of…concerned. He was based in south Florida for a while, and ever since he came back, I've had the feeling something is wrong."

"Have you asked him?"

"Yes, and he's politely told me to mind my own business." She smiled. "Well, I'm his baby sister. He always thinks he has to be the big responsible one with the rest of us. Maybe he'll talk to you."

That jolted her down to her soles, and for a moment she couldn't find the breath to reply. "Why would he talk to me?" Her voice didn't sound natural, even to her.

Georgia shrugged, not meeting her gaze. "Oh, I don't know. He just seems different with you than with most people. It's hard to say, but sometimes you have a rapport with someone. Seems like Adam's that way with you. Anyway, if he mentions it, don't you tell him I said anything."

"I won't." It seemed highly unlikely that the subject would ever come up, so it was an easy promise to make.

As for rapport—well, maybe there was something between her and Adam, but it was just that they'd been forced into a situation where they'd had to rely on each other to get her grandfather to

admit the truth and to get her here. That was all—
that and the attraction that Adam had been so quick
to put aside.

Chapter Six

Cathy had planned to stay at the house this afternoon and help Delia with the preparations for the family party tonight. Instead, she found herself walking down a sandy path around the beach house, following Adam, who had Jamie on his shoulder.

She wasn't quite sure how it had happened, except that Jamie could talk of nothing else since that glimpse he had of the ocean when they'd been on the island with Georgia yesterday. For whatever reason, his constant chatter seemed to annoy Grandpa, so she hadn't objected too hard when Delia decided to shoo them out of the house that afternoon.

It couldn't be too comfortable for Adam to carry Jamie, with those metal braces bumping against his chest, but it didn't deter him. He was looking up at Jamie, laughing at something, and the expression on Jamie's face made her heart stop.

A fierce longing swept through her to have that for Jamie—a strong man to carry him, to make him laugh, to show him how to grow up into a good person.

She pushed the thought away just as fiercely. It wasn't likely to happen. Just look at how Adam had reacted, stepping away so quickly after he'd kissed her. That should tell her all she needed to know.

Adam lowered Jamie to the sand next to a long, shallow pool. "Tide's going out, giving us a nice, warm tidal pool for Jamie's first experience." He flipped out the blanket he carried and spread it on the sand. "Just put that cooler on the corner to keep the blanket flat, will you?"

She set the small cooler of drinks down where he indicated, putting her beach bag on the opposite corner. The beach stretched out in both directions, shining where the waves washed it. A few family groups were dotted here and there, but not nearly as many as she'd expected.

"It's fairly quiet," she said.

Adam shrugged, pulling off his shirt and shedding his shoes. "It is September, after all. Kids get busy with school things, I guess, even on the weekends. We were like that, I remember. Couldn't get enough of the beach all summer long, but once school started and fall sports, we'd kind of forget, I guess." He turned to Jamie. "So, what do you think,

Jamie? Shall we get rid of the shoes and braces and go in the tidal pool?"

"Is it okay, Mama?" Jamie hung back, a bit awed, she thought.

She found she was looking up at Adam, shading her eyes with her hand. "You're sure it's safe?"

He laughed. "Safe? What wouldn't be safe about a tidal pool? You can see clear to the bottom."

"Right. Yes." He made her feel like an idiot, but this was nearly as new to her as it was to Jamie. "Come on, Jamie. Let's get some sunscreen on."

Peeling off his shirt, she rubbed him well with the lotion, then removed the braces.

Adam already stood calf-deep in water. "In you come, Jamie." He held out his hands.

Without a moment of hesitation, Jamie grabbed them and went in the water. A delighted smile spread over his face. "It's warm, Mama."

"Just like a bath," Adam assured him. "That's how the water is in September. Now, where did we put those boats we brought?"

Cathy fetched the boats and settled herself on the blanket to watch. Jamie clearly didn't need her. He played quite happily with Adam, racing the boats around and making the vrooming noises so popular with small boys.

She should not be sitting here thinking about how the sun reflected off Adam's tanned skin and picked out glints of gold in his brown hair. She tilted the sunhat Delia had lent her a little further down her forehead, as if that might block him out.

Finally Adam came out of the water, dropping onto the blanket next to her. "He's enjoying it."

"He is, isn't he? It's all he's talked about since yesterday, until I thought he'd drive Grandpa crazy."

"Still no clue as to why your grandfather is reacting that way to the ocean?"

She shook her head. "He's been so contented that I haven't wanted to bring up anything that might cause him to get upset. Maybe he'll tell Miz Callie."

"He might. Folks do have a way of telling her things."

Was that another jab at her for talking to Miz Callie about Jamie, instead of him? Maybe, but he didn't seem to be doing anything but stating a fact.

"He seems to have taken quite a shine to your father, as well as to Miz Callie."

"Another oldest son," Adam commented. "Maybe he sees himself in him."

"Maybe so."

She'd never really thought of her grandfather in relation to his birth family, because he'd never spoken of them until Adam came into their lives. Had he taken special pride in being the oldest? If so, the problems with his father must have been especially hurtful.

She glanced at the beach house behind them. Its tan shingles seemed to blend into the surrounding dunes and sea oats, looking as if it had grown there.

"You said that Grandpa was living here at the time of the quarrel with his father?"

Adam nodded. "The family always moved out to the beach house for the summer. The way I hear it, Ned's father declared that not even Hitler was going to keep him from doing what he always did."

It was hard to picture her grandfather growing up in the shadow of the war. "I can't imagine what it was like then."

"You should get Miz Callie to talk about it. She remembers those days well, especially the summer of '42, when Ned left. Half the island was taken over by the military, and German subs were trying to sink shipping right out there." He nodded off to the horizon, where the ocean met the sky.

She shivered a little in spite of the warmth of the sun. "So your family has had the beach house for a long time?"

"My granddad's grandfather, or maybe it was great-grandfather, owned a lot of land out here. It was granddad's father who built the house, I think, and gradually sold off some lots to other people. I'm not real clear on all that history, to tell the truth.

I just got interested when Miz Callie started the search for Ned. You ask her about it. She loves to talk about stuff like that."

"I will."

Adam was frustratingly vague, but what he'd said made it clear that the family had owned property at the time her grandfather's father was presumably making out a will. He'd left it all to someone. To Adam's grandfather, maybe, if he'd thought Ned was dead. But if he hadn't…

"What say I take Jamie in the waves for a bit?" Adam's question chased everything else out of her mind. "It's dead calm right now, so that's a good first time."

"I don't know." She looked at the ocean with a certain amount of wariness. True, the waves were mere ripples where they retreated, but farther out the swells looked a bit scary.

"It's safe," he said, seeming impatient with her hesitation.

"Okay, if he wants to. But don't take him out very far."

She had the sense that Adam barely refrained from rolling his eyes. He splashed back into the tidal pool to Jamie.

"What do you say, Jamie? Want to go out in the waves? I'll carry you, if you want."

Jamie was already struggling to his feet before Adam finished talking. "Yes, sir!"

"Good man." Adam scooped him up and strode through the tidal pool toward the shining wet sand beyond.

Cathy hurried after them. She shouldn't be so nervous about this. Adam and his family treated the ocean like a second backyard, it seemed.

Jamie didn't seem to share her apprehension. As soon as Adam was out to his knees, he was wiggling to be put down. She waded in a bit, trying to get used to the feel of the sand sliding away under her feet as the waves moved in and out.

"Look at me, Mama. I'm swimming!" Jamie swung his arms wildly. With a quick twist, he spun free of Adam's hands just as a wave hit. He disappeared under the murky green water.

Panic shot through her. She plunged toward him, staggering as she tried to run through the surf. "Jamie!"

As quickly as it had happened, it was over. Adam scooped Jamie up in his arms, smiling a little. "Hey, buddy, you're not supposed to drink the ocean."

Jamie sputtered, rubbing his eyes with his fists, his face white. Before he could respond she reached him, snatching him away from Adam.

She held him close, feeling him shiver as the breeze hit his wet skin. "Jamie, are you all right? Are you hurt?" She could hear the fear in her voice. She tried to quell it, but that moment when he'd disappeared under the surface…

"Mama." He put his arms around her neck and buried his face in her neck.

"Don't overreact," Adam said quietly. "You'll make him think it's something to be afraid of."

She glared at him, holding her child close. "You said you'd take care of him. You let go of him. Don't you realize he could have been hurt?"

His face seemed to whiten under his tan, and lines bracketed his mouth. "He's not hurt. You're making too much of this."

Jamie, maybe feeling the tension between them, clung even harder, beginning to cry.

"It's all right, sugar." She patted him. "Come on, now. I think it's time we got dried off."

"Cathy, it's not a good idea to end on a bad note."

Maybe she had overreacted just a bit, but she wasn't about to admit it to him. "I think I'm the best judge of what's right for my son," she said stiffly.

"Right. Fine." He started toward the beach. "If that's how you want it."

Holding Jamie close, she stumbled after him. That wasn't just how she wanted it. That was how it had to be.

Adam had been trying to forget his annoyance with Cathy during most of the family party that night. He wasn't succeeding.

She'd made him feel guilty, but then, he'd probably feel guilty without any help from her.

Even so, Cathy had been wrong. She wouldn't admit it. She had to be everything to her son—that was obvious.

He watched her from his perch on the low stone wall that surrounded his mother's rose garden. Most of the party had moved outside after the meal was over, some still hanging on to dessert plates or glasses of sweet tea.

People circulated, everyone making an effort to talk to the newcomers. If Cathy was finding it a trial, she seemed to be hiding it well. She was talking to his cousin Amanda at the moment— or, rather, she was listening. Amanda seemed to be doing the talking for both of them. That was Amanda, endlessly interested in everyone and everything. No wonder she'd ended up being a reporter.

Ned, with Miz Callie next to him introducing people, seemed to be coping. If he was a little brusque, they would understand.

Jamie and Lindsay were sitting on a blanket under the grape arbor, playing a game Lindsay had brought along. He wandered over, squatting down next to them.

"Hey, you two. Did you get enough to eat?"

Lindsay grinned. "I sure did. It was awesome."

He smiled, giving her ponytail a gentle tug.

"You're looking more grown-up all the time, Miz Lindsay." He turned to Jamie. "How you feeling, Jamie? All over your duck in the ocean?"

"I reckon so." Jamie's eyes slid away from his. "I wasn't scared. Not really."

"I'm sure of that." Poor kid probably didn't want Adam thinking he was a baby just because his mother treated him that way.

"I've been ducked lots of times," Lindsay said. "One time a wave caught me and turned me clear upside down. What you have to do, see, is close your eyes and hold your breath, like this." She squinted her eyes shut and sucked in her breath, face turning red with effort.

"Okay, that's enough." He patted her back to get her to release the breath. "Jamie gets it now."

Jamie nodded, looking impressed with his newfound cousin's abilities.

Adam rose, smiling a little at the way their relationship was developing. Even though they weren't blood kin, that was no reason they couldn't be cousins.

He wandered back to his stone wall, figuring that was as good a spot as any to pretend he wasn't watching Cathy. He spotted his cousin Win coming out the French doors carrying a plate with not one, but two slices of pecan pie.

"Look at that boy." Hugh sat down next to him.

"Two pieces of pie—and there's not an ounce of fat on him."

"He's younger than we are," Adam reminded him. "And rescue swimmers expend a lot of calories just training, let alone when they're out on a mission."

Hugh nodded, silent for a moment. He was probably remembering, as Adam was, that time a couple of months ago when Win had been missing out on the ocean, supporting two survivors of a boating accident until help could get there.

"Looks like everyone's had a chance to talk to the new relatives," Hugh said. "They seem to be holding up pretty well under all the attention."

"Right. Your sister is monopolizing Cathy, I see."

"You want me to tell her to move on so you can have a chance?" Hugh asked.

"Cathy's not too interested in talking to me right now, I'd guess. She's still mad at me just because Jamie got a mouthful of sea water when we were out at the beach today."

"Shucks, if I had a nickel for every gallon of sea water I swallowed as a kid, I'd be a rich man today. She shouldn't baby the boy."

It was what he'd been thinking, but he found himself wanting to defend her anyway. "We were brought up around it—sea water in our veins, most likely. She wasn't."

"Even so—"

"And Jamie's problems might make her a little overprotective."

Hugh raised an eyebrow. "Sounds like you're a little defensive on the subject of Cathy Norwood. You still think there's more going on than the obvious?"

"I don't know." Adam wasn't sure he could sort out objective facts from the complicated feelings mother and son roused in him. "We were at the beach house this afternoon."

When he stopped, Hugh nudged him. "Yeah, right, I got that part. You were at the beach house and what?"

"She asked a lot of questions." He tried to analyze it in his own mind. "Maybe it's natural enough, but it seemed like she was awfully interested in the property. How long it had been in the family, stuff like that. I don't know—it just didn't feel quite right to me."

Hugh mused for a moment, his expression even more wooden than usual. Now it was Adam's turn to nudge. "You falling asleep there?"

"No. Just thinking that it might be worthwhile to be a little discreet looking into Mrs. Cathy Norwood. Catherine? Or Cathleen?"

"Cathleen," he said. "But listen, she and her grandfather can't know you're doing anything of the kind."

Hugh gave him a pitying look. "What do you take me for, an amateur? Of course they won't know."

"What do you expect to find?" He was the one unleashing this, and he wasn't so sure it was a good idea.

"That's the thing. You never know what you're going to find until you look." Hugh studied his face for a moment. "Listen, it's your call, okay? You've been around them the most. But if there's any doubt, well, Miz Callie comes first."

Miz Callie did come first, even though this felt a lot like betrayal.

"Okay. Better do it. Just, please, be discreet."

"Will do." Hugh gave him a mock salute and wandered off.

Probably to get himself another piece of pie, Adam thought bitterly. Leaving him with nothing to feast on but an extra load of guilt.

He ought to be used to that by now.

Coming back downstairs after putting Jamie to bed, Cathy realized she'd been gone longer than she thought. Jamie had been overexcited and naturally reluctant to leave all these fascinating new cousins.

She was relieved to see that the crowd of Bodines had thinned out considerably. It had taken her an hour to sort them all out, and just when she thought she had them, she'd discovered that the woman she was talking to was Amanda Bodine, rather than her twin sister, Annabel.

Well, at least now it was down to a manageable group of people she knew. They'd gathered in the family room. Grandpa sat in the rocker he'd adopted as "his" chair, with Miz Callie sitting nearby. Georgia, Adam, Adam's parents—they were still talking, as if they were as reluctant to see the evening end as Jamie had been.

Adam was watching her. The knowledge made her awkward as she crossed the room and found a seat a safe distance away from him.

The quick flame of anger she'd felt with him earlier in the day had long since cooled to ash. He'd meant well. She knew that. He just didn't understand what it was like to care for a child like Jamie.

The hum of conversation gradually died out, leaving an air of expectation in the room. Cathy's nerves prickled. Had they been waiting for her to come back down? Why? She shot a glance at Adam to find that he was still watching her, eyes steady, face unreadable.

Miz Callie leaned forward to put her hand on Grandpa's arm. Cathy felt everyone's attention sharpen, as if the simple gesture had been a signal.

"Ned, there's something we've been wanting to

tell you." She smiled a little, as if at herself. "Truth to tell, I've been holding off on it, thinking it might make you mad at me for prying."

Grandpa gave her the indulgent look that he seemed to reserve for her and Jamie. "Don't reckon you could do anything that bad, little Callie."

Something caught at Cathy's heart. He used to look at her that way, talk to her in that tone that seemed to forgive everything.

"We'll see if you feel that way once you hear what we have to say." Miz Callie's blue eyes were filled with compassion. "You see, when we started trying to learn what happened to you and why you left, we found out about Grace Malloy."

Grace Malloy? The name meant nothing to her, but it obviously seemed to mean something to Grandpa. He looked—well, vulnerable. That was the only word she could think of.

She leaned forward. Should she intervene?

Almost as if he'd felt her thought, Adam rose. He moved casually across the room, set his coffee cup on the mantel, and took the seat next to her. Her nerves jangled, and she took a steadying breath.

"How did you—" Grandpa stopped, as if not sure he wanted to know the answer.

"As I thought about that summer, the memories started to come back." Miz Callie patted his arm. "You know how it is. Sometimes those old memories are sharper and clearer than something that happened last week."

Grandpa nodded, surprising Cathy. He never talked to her about the past, but apparently he thought about it.

"Georgia did most of the work, with Matt's help," Miz Callie said. "So maybe she should tell you about it."

Georgia's color rose a little at becoming the center of attention. "Everyone we talked to seemed to remember different things about that summer, but one story would trigger something else. Eventually we realized that they all centered around the same person."

Grandpa grunted, not looking at her, and Cathy's hand clenched on the arm of the chair. If this was going to upset him, they should have told her about it first. Maybe they figured that since they were blood kin and she wasn't, they had the right to make decisions.

"Grace was a lovely young woman," Miz Callie said softly. "And her husband was abusive. Richmond and I—we knew, but we didn't understand what it was we knew."

Grandpa nodded, his hands tightening into fists, the veins standing out like blue cords. "She deserved better."

"Even Miz Callie's little sister, Lizbet, remembered something that helped to piece it all together,"

Georgia said. "Do you remember the night you pulled Mrs. Malloy out of the surf?"

Grandpa nodded. He put his hand up to his eyes, as if to shade them. "I forgot Lizbet was there that night. Grace—she'd have killed herself if I hadn't been there."

"That was why you felt you had to stay on the island, to try to help her," Miz Callie said gently. "You put your plans to enlist on hold, but your daddy didn't understand."

Grandpa's head came up, his eyes flashing. "Thought I was a coward. My own father. The quarrels…seemed like they'd never end."

Cathy's heart clenched. He might have been talking about the two of them, when she'd told him she loved Paul Norwood and wanted to leave school. Those quarrels had been unending, too.

"Finally you knew that you couldn't change anything. You wrote to Grace, telling her you were going to enlist under another name," Georgia said.

Georgia's words had Grandpa swiveling to face her. "How do you know that?" His voice was harsh. "Did you talk to her?"

"By the time we found her, she wasn't able to talk." Georgia's lips trembled, and she pressed them together for a moment before she continued. "She passed away shortly afterward, but her daughter gave me the letters you wrote to her." She passed a handful of envelopes to him, the ink so badly faded it was barely legible. "I guess these belong to you, now."

The decades-old story seemed alive in the room. Cathy's heart ached for those young lovers, living out their own tragedy against the background of a war that changed so many young lives.

Grandpa sat motionless, staring down at the letters in his hand. A tear dropped on the topmost envelope.

Cathy thought her heart would break for him. Grandpa never cried, even when Grandma died, at least not where anyone could see him.

She went to him, putting her arms around him gently, half expecting him to push her away, as he usually did.

Not this time. He turned his face against her shoulder, much as Jamie would, and she felt his shoulders shake.

"I hope we weren't wrong to tell you." Miz Callie stroked his arm in sympathy. "We thought you should know."

Grandpa drew away a little, but he held tight to Cathy's hand. "It's right. I should know." He looked up at her then. "Help me up to my room, child."

Nodding, Cathy put her arm around him. One thing, at least, had come from this. Grandpa was turning to her again willingly, and she was grateful.

Chapter Seven

Miz Callie linked her arm with Cathy's as they walked along the tree-shaded sidewalk to church the next day. "Often I attend services on the island, but this congregation in Mount Pleasant is really the home church for the Bodines."

"It's a beautiful building." The graceful white Colonial church didn't look large enough to hold all the people streaming toward it.

"I'm glad your grandfather wanted to come this morning." Miz Callie squeezed her arm, as if the two of them should be happy together.

She wasn't sure whether happy was the right word. Apprehensive might be a better choice. What if being in the church, with all its memories of his life before the war, upset Grandpa? After his tears the previous night, she'd found herself lying awake, worrying. She'd expected his reconciliation with his family to be a happy event, but it seemed to be stirring up all sorts of other emotions.

Delia, who was walking ahead of them with Jamie by the hand, glanced back over her shoulder. "Cathy, is it all right if Jamie goes to children's church? They have such a nice program." She smiled down at Jamie. "You'd like to go with the other children, wouldn't you?"

"Yes, ma'am. Can I, Mama?"

"May I," she correctly automatically. The word *no* hovered on the tip of her tongue.

But Jamie was looking at her with such enthusiasm in his eyes, and Adam, standing next to his mother, had an expression that was equally easy to read.

He thought she was overprotective. He'd made that very clear. If she refused to let Jamie attend something as benign as children's church, he'd just be confirmed in his belief.

"I guess that would be all right. Where—"

"I'll take you." Adam lifted Jamie, braces and all. "You're going to like this." He cut across the grass to a brick building next to the sanctuary, and she followed him.

Double doors stood open. Adam walked inside, not even making a pretence of waiting for her, and she hurried her steps.

"I'll take him in—" she began, but Adam was already setting Jamie down.

"The kindergarten-age room is right over there." He pointed across the hall. "I figured he wanted to walk in under his own steam."

She nodded, reluctant to admit that Adam had good instincts. Jamie, not reluctant at all about this, headed straight for the door.

Cathy paused in the doorway. A middle-aged woman whose youthful face and sparkling eyes belied her gray hair came quickly to greet them. Smiling, she knelt to offer her hand to Jamie. "Hi, there. I'm Miz Sally. What's your name?"

"Jamie Norwood, ma'am." Jamie shook hands gravely.

"Welcome, Jamie. You come right over here to the clay table. We could use some help making animals for Noah's Ark, okay?"

"Okay." Jamie took her hand and went off without a backward glance.

Cathy felt a little bereft. Of course she wanted him to be comfortable in new situations, but…

"Looks like he's happy," Adam said. "Shall we join the others?"

She nodded, managing a stiff smile, and walked back outside with him.

"You know, I think I remember making clay animals for Noah's Ark when I was in that room," Adam said, moving quickly to where the others waited. "I'll just make sure Uncle Ned can manage the steps."

He left her abruptly, going to take Grandpa's arm. To her relief, Grandpa accepted the help. He went up the three shallow steps to the door with Adam on one side and Adam's father on the other.

"Don't worry." Miz Callie said the words too softly for Grandpa to hear. "He did want to come, remember."

Miz Callie seemed to have a habit of reading people's thoughts.

"I know. I just hope it doesn't upset him."

Miz Callie patted her arm with a feather-light touch. "You want to protect the people you love. That does you credit. But maybe sometimes we need to be upset."

"I don't think—"

"There have been times when God took my peaceful life, turned it upside down and shook it. Maybe it seemed like the worst thing in the world at the time, but as long as I kept leaning on Him, something good came of it in the end."

Before Cathy could respond, they were entering the church. There was a small vestibule, and then double doors opened to the sanctuary.

Ashton and Delia led the way down the center aisle, followed by Grandpa, leaning a little on Adam's arm. She and Miz Callie brought up the rear.

The sanctuary gave an instant atmosphere of reverence. High-ceilinged, it had balconies around three sides and old-fashioned closed pews. Most of the glass in the windows was clear, rather than stained, filling the space with light.

Apparently the Bodines sat near the front. If she'd come in on her own, she'd have slipped into the first empty pew in the rear, not walked the length of the nave.

People were watching them. No one was rude enough to stare, but she still caught the curious glances. Her cheeks heated. Everyone here had probably already heard some version of the return of Ned Bodine to his family after all these years. Their interest was understandable, but she was still relieved to sit down.

Until she realized that Adam had maneuvered their seating. She had Grandpa on one side of her and Adam on the other. He probably meant well, thinking he'd keep her with her grandfather. He didn't realize they were the two people most likely to keep her emotions in turmoil.

The organist came to the end of a crashing piece, the bell tolled, and the service began. Cathy composed her face and folded her hands.

Grandpa seemed fine. She could ignore Adam, and she was fine, too. Right up until the moment when the Old Testament scripture was read.

"The eternal God is thy refuge, and underneath are the everlasting arms." The minister read the short verse from Deuteronomy slowly, his deep voice lingering over the words like a bell tolling.

That bell seemed to resound through her, and she heard again Miz Callie's words about how she'd leaned on God.

It wasn't—she didn't mean Cathy, surely. She didn't know anything about Cathy's spiritual state. She couldn't know how Cathy had responded to the double blow of learning her beautiful baby was seriously disabled and watching her husband walk away.

Tears prickled against Cathy's eyelids, and she struggled to blink them away. She had turned to God then, hadn't she? She'd begged, demanded, pleaded.

But she hadn't stayed close. She hadn't leaned on those everlasting arms.

The tears wouldn't stop. As quickly as she blinked away one, another formed. She grabbed her bag, scrabbling futilely for a tissue.

She'd worried that Grandpa would get emotional, but she was the one who was going to make a fool of herself.

Adam's hand moved against hers. Without turning his face away from the minister, he shoved a handkerchief into her hand. He squeezed her fingers, just once, and then he took his hand away.

Just once, but it was enough to squeeze her heart, too.

* * *

"You just enjoy yourself, now." Adam's father, Ashton, paused on the sidewalk outside the public garage in downtown Charleston where he'd just parked. "My meeting will run until two o'clock at least, longer if the speaker is long-winded. If you're not here when I come out, I'll wait in the car. You just enjoy your walk around the historic district."

"Yes, sir, I'm sure I will. Thank you so much for bringing me." At least, she'd enjoy it if she accomplished what she intended.

"No trouble at all." Ashton raised his hand in farewell and marched off down the block to his luncheon meeting on Charleston military history. With his brisk stride and military bearing, there was no doubt that he belonged there. He had a shock of thick graying hair and a lined, distinguished face that made her think of a judge. Calm, judicious, deliberate—those were nice qualities. Adam was like his father in that way.

She consulted the tourist map Delia had given her and turned right. The building she sought was at the corner of Broad Street and Meeting Street, so it shouldn't be more than a couple of blocks.

The Bodines thought she wanted a quiet walk around the historic district. The guilt that was becoming too familiar swept over her again. She was deceiving people who'd been nothing but kind to her, but what else could she do? She could hardly say that she was headed to the Charleston courthouse to check out Grandpa's father's will.

She walked quickly, too intent on her task to give more than a superficial look at the historic buildings that surrounded her. She'd been studying this area on the framed map of the city that hung in the study of the Bodine house, trying to figure out how on earth she was going to get there without anyone knowing. Ashton and Adam walked in on her, and Ashton immediately assumed that she wanted to tour the historic district. He was going to that very place for a lecture, and what could be easier? Delia would be delighted to look after her grandfather and Jamie for a bit, so that she could have a little outing.

The whole thing had arranged itself so easily that it bothered her. She wasn't used to having something she wanted come without effort.

Adam hadn't said anything while his mother and father were making arrangements. He'd stood back, watching. Suspiciously, it seemed to her. Things had deteriorated between them, and she didn't know how to fix that, or even if she should. Maybe this estrangement was better for both of them.

She rounded the corner, and there it was. The white, Federal-style courthouse stood as a mute reminder that Charleston had once aspired to be the state capitol. She'd learned that doing a Web search on Ashton's computer. More importantly, she'd learned that wills probated prior to 1983 were stored on microfilm at the historic courthouse.

She crossed the street, dodging a line of camera-laden tourists following a guide. If she found the will… A flutter of excitement went through her. Not just excitement. Hope. Suppose Grandfather was mentioned in his father's will?

It could be. His father hadn't known whether Ned was dead or alive. If he had left Grandpa something, even a token amount, that could make all the difference in their lives.

For a brief moment, as she passed into the building, she indulged in a dream—the family happily giving Grandpa his rightful share, Jamie having surgery, their lives suddenly easier.

She stopped in the hallway, consulting the building directory. Dreams were dangerous. Dreams could make you believe in happy endings. The only happy ending she wanted was to see her son walk and run like any other child. Finding out the terms of the will was the next step toward achieving that.

The estate division was on the third floor. She had the date of death, thanks to the elaborate family tree which Delia had shown her. Five minutes later she held the microfilm in her hands. She sat down at a viewer and tried to decipher the directions.

"Can I give you a hand with that, ma'am?" The

assistant who stood behind her chair was so young that surely he must be a student intern.

She surrendered the microfilm and watched him set it up effortlessly.

"Thank you so much. That's very kind of you."

"A pleasure, ma'am." He ducked his head, flushing a little.

She should have been able to do it herself. She'd certainly done research in college. But that was a lifetime ago, and skills grew rusty with disuse. She could can tomatoes with the best of them, but she wasn't much use in a library anymore.

The young man glanced at the name and death date she'd written down and scrolled quickly to the page. Her breath caught when she saw it appear on the screen in front of her.

"Would you like me to make you a photocopy?" The boy leaned against the partition that separated the machines. "I can do that easily while you're looking. There's just a small charge for that."

This was even better than she'd hoped. "Yes, please."

He hurried off, maybe glad to have something to do. The estate division wasn't exactly a hotbed of activity at the moment.

Taking a deep breath, she settled down to read. *Please,* she found herself murmuring.

The legal preliminaries took some time to plod through, but at last she found it.

"…to my sole surviving son, Richmond Bodine, I leave all…"

She didn't bother to read more. Disappointment was a heavy weight in her stomach. Everything had been left to Adam's grandfather. Nothing to hers.

Sole surviving son. The words tasted bitter. He hadn't been the sole surviving son. Grandpa was alive. Didn't he deserve something?

By 1950, when the will was written, his father must have believed Ned to be deceased. Was there anything to be made of that, legally? She hadn't the faintest idea, but her dream of an easy happy ending fizzled away to nothing.

When her young friend returned with the copy, she paid for it and slid it into her bag. She didn't know what good it would do, but maybe she'd think of something.

She took a more leisurely route back to the parking garage, making a point of admiring some of the buildings Delia had marked on the map. Her heart really wasn't in sightseeing, but they would ask. She had to have something to tell them.

By the time she approached the parking garage again, her feet were a bit the worse for wear. Sandals were not ideal for walking on cobblestones. Worse still was the disappointment that pressed down on her. What was she going to do next? She might not have much time. Grandpa could decide at any moment to go home, and they'd be back in the same place again, with nothing to show for the trip but a brief encounter with a life they could never hope to have.

She hurried along the sidewalk when she glimpsed a figure waiting outside the parking garage. But it wasn't Ashton. It was Adam, imposing in dress blues, and he was clearly waiting for her.

A surge of pleasure caught Adam by surprise when he saw Cathy striding down the street toward him. Then his brain clicked into gear. He reminded himself of why he'd come, and it certainly wasn't to gawk at the way Cathy's soft skirt fluttered around her legs.

Still, he couldn't help but notice how much better she looked after even the short time she'd been here. She seemed years younger than the wary, tired creature he'd encountered in the dusty garden.

Her hair was loose around her shoulders, and the breeze teased tendrils around a face that had softened, somehow. It wasn't quite as taut against the bone as it had been that day. If he saw her for the first time now, he'd give her an appreciative second look.

She hadn't lost the wariness, however. He could see that in her face as soon as she realized that he was the one waiting for her.

He reminded himself to smile casually as she approached. "Hey, Cathy."

"What's wrong? Your father…"

"Nothing's wrong. Why would you think that?"

She came to a stop a few feet away, frowning a bit, her hand fiddling with the strap of her shoulder bag. "I…I don't know. I guess because he said he'd meet me, and instead here you are, looking all formal and solemn."

A car swung out of the garage, narrowly missing them, and he took her arm to move her away a few feet. "This is a bad place to wait. Daddy's going to be another half hour. Some historian he just had to chat with, so he told me to keep you occupied 'til he's ready to go. Why don't we walk over to Washington Park?"

She resisted the gentle pressure of his hand. "I'll be fine waiting for your father. There's no need for you to stay with me."

Her response triggered that annoying little edge of suspicion he couldn't quite dismiss. Why was she so eager to be rid of him?

Maybe she just doesn't like your company, a wry voice commented in the back of his mind. *Nothin' so suspicious about that, is there?*

"I told my daddy I'd hang around until he's done. You don't want to make a liar out of me."

He nudged her gently. "Come on. The park's nicer than a parking garage, I promise."

With an air of giving in to the inevitable, she fell into step beside him. "I didn't realize you were coming to the luncheon." She gave a sideways glance at his uniform. "And all dressed up, too."

"Don't remind me. But it pleases my father, and it's not as if I was far away." He gestured behind them. "If you went down Broad Street that way until you met the Ashley River, you'd find Coast Guard Base Charleston."

She glanced back in the direction of his gesture. "I didn't realize the base was right downtown. So you came because you wanted to please your daddy, not from some deep interest in military history?"

"It's his passion, with the result that we've had it drummed into us from the time we could talk."

Along with some other maxims to live by. Duty first, honor above all. A good officer is always fair. That was really why he was here. Trying to be fair to Cathy, though she didn't know it.

Something had been off about that conversation with his father yesterday, when they'd found her in the study, poring over the map of Charleston. She'd looked like a kid with her hand caught in the cookie jar. He couldn't believe Daddy hadn't seen that, but he'd been as smooth as could be, assuming she wanted to see the historic district and giving her a golden opportunity to do that.

So she'd had her chance. What had she done with it? Or was he letting Hugh's law-enforcement attitude infect him, seeing mysteries where there weren't any?

They'd reached Washington Park, and he led her to a convenient bench under the dappled shade of a massive live oak. When he sat down next to her, she plopped that oversize shoulder bag of hers between them on the seat, for all the world like a barrier.

His lips twitched. Did she think he was going to make a pass right out here in public? Or maybe that gesture was a bit more subtle, showing her determination not to let him in on whatever she'd been doing.

"Did you have a nice walk? What did you see?" Maybe he wasn't so awfully subtle himself, but if she really had been sightseeing, she'd have some answers.

"Lots of beautiful old houses," she said promptly. "And I have a question for you, since you're a native. Why are they turned sideways?"

Either she really was curious, or she'd hit on a way of distracting him from what she hadn't done with her couple of hours in the city. An officer is always fair, he reminded himself. Trouble was, he usually didn't have his emotions in the balance.

"Well, now, you've hit on a question that would keep Daddy's historians busy for years, if they weren't so obsessed with refighting the battle of

Fort Sumter. Those houses are called single houses, and you'll find them all over the old part of the city." He spotted one just across the street and pointed. "See how it's laid out. It's just one room wide on the side that faces the street. Then it goes back as deep as the homeowner could afford to build. There's a door onto the street, but the house really faces to the side, where the piazza opens onto the garden."

She nodded, leaning forward to stare at the building between the passing cars. "But why? Why doesn't it face the street?"

"One theory says it's because homeowners were taxed based on the amount of street frontage they had. Others say the style is meant to catch the sea breezes. Then there are passionate defenders of the idea that the building lots were divided and divided again as fathers left property to their sons."

She stiffened. She was close enough that he could feel the tension, but he had no idea what caused it.

"Why fathers to sons?" Her voice seemed a little sharper than the question warranted. "I mean, didn't the daughters get anything?" Maybe she'd realized she was giving something away, because the second question came out with a kind of forced lightness.

"We're talking eighteenth century here," he said.

"Property generally stayed in the male line. Maybe they didn't want it going out of the family."

She closed her lips on something she'd been about to say and smiled instead. "Sounds very paternalistic," she said lightly. She glanced at her watch. "Should we check to see if your father is ready?"

"There's no hurry. Not on his part, anyway. Like I said, once they start refighting old battles, they don't know when to quit. Tell me what else you saw. Did you make it as far down as the Edmondston-Alston House?"

"I…I don't think so." She looked momentarily confused. "All those names—that's not one of the house museums on Meeting Street, is it?"

"No, it's down on the Battery." The sheer wealth of restored houses could be confusing to an outsider, he supposed. "My cousin Amanda lives in a restored gatehouse down that way. You might have run into her if you went that way. Charleston's a small city."

"I'd love to see more of the historic district sometime." She fidgeted with the strap of her bag. "Don't you think we should be getting back?"

What was she so nervous about? He decided on a direct attack. "Why did you really want to come downtown today, Cathy? It wasn't historic houses, was it?"

"I don't know what you mean." Her words denied

it, but her hand jerked on the strap of her bag, sending it toppling off the bench and onto the grass.

He bent automatically to help gather things up. A tired joke about the contents of women's bags died on his lips as a sheaf of paper unfolded in his hand. It took a moment before his mind processed what he was looking at. It was a copy of his great-grandfather's will.

He clenched it, shock stiffening his muscles. He had to wait a moment before he could trust himself to speak. "I guess I know now why you came downtown, don't I? Where did you—the courthouse, I suppose. That's where wills are on file."

"That's right." Her tone was defiant, but her gaze slid away from his. "It's public knowledge. Anyone can go in and look at probated wills."

"Not just anyone would have an interest in my great-grandfather's will. Not just anyone would lie about what she was doing today."

Her face paled, and she sucked in a breath as if he'd hit her. "I'm sorry about that part of it. I didn't want to lie."

"Then why did you?" Underneath his anger was honest bewilderment. "What do you want?"

"I want…I have to protect my grandfather and my son. They're my responsibility." Passion flooded her face with renewed color, making her almost beautiful. "Don't you understand that? If my grandfather had been owed something under the terms of his father's will, I had to know, whether that makes you think less of me or not."

The fair-officer part of him understood that, even though not approving of her secrecy. He could even admit that she had no more reason to trust them than they did to trust her. But at a strictly human level, he was hurt. Betrayed.

"Since you've seen the will, you know the answer to your question. The property was left to my granddad."

Probably by that time Granddad's father believed Ned had died, since they hadn't heard from him in so long. If he hadn't, if he'd had some reason to believe Ned was still alive, would he have written the will some other way? Adam didn't know the answer to that.

"Yes. I know." She stood, not looking at him. "I think we'd better go back."

"Cathy." He reached out, almost touching her, and then drew his hand back. "If there's anything else you want to know, ask Miz Callie. She'll tell you the truth. She puts a high value on that."

Her cheeks flamed again, but she nodded.

He'd almost said, ask me. That would be useless. She clearly didn't trust him.

And he didn't trust her. He'd wanted to know what she was up to this afternoon, and he'd found out, all right. But it just made the whole situation more difficult.

Chapter Eight

Adam squinted out at the green, rolling waves. His mind ought to be on this patrol run. Ought to be. Unfortunately, it kept straying off to the situation with Cathy.

Their patrol had been routine, so far. Routine gave him too much time to think.

He still hadn't come to terms with Cathy's actions. It wasn't so much her wanting to know how the property had been left. Calculating as that sounded, he could understand that.

He'd seen how close to the bone she and her grandfather lived, to say nothing of Jamie's special needs. If Adam were in that situation, he'd be looking for any way out, too, even a long-shot inheritance from a distant relative.

It was how she'd gone about it that got under his skin. The lies—well, technically she hadn't lied, he supposed. She just hadn't volunteered that she wanted to do something in addition to looking at houses downtown.

Still, she hadn't trusted him. She didn't trust anyone else, either.

That lack of trust—was it because she'd been hurt too often? Or was it because she had something to hide? He didn't know, and he needed to.

He'd been tempted to spill the whole thing to his father, but something had held him back. Daddy would be fair—he didn't doubt that. But once he knew, how hard would it be to look at Cathy in the same way? What family upheaval might it cause if Daddy decided he had to talk to Cathy and her grandfather about her actions? He didn't know, so in the end, he'd kept it to himself.

"Take a look." Jim Masters jogged his elbow and handed him a pair of binoculars. "That seem right to you?"

Adam took the binoculars and focused in on what he should have seen first, if he hadn't been focusing on personal problems instead of work. It was a high-powered speedboat, probably a twenty-footer.

"Changed course when they spotted us," Jim said. "A go-fast?"

Slang for smugglers in a fast boat. "They're a little too far out to be your average pleasure boat." He knew exactly what Jim was thinking, and Terry Loudon, too. The three of them had worked together long enough that they didn't need a lot of talk to understand each other. "Let's see what happens when we try to close up on them."

Terry nodded, sending the forty-one-foot utility boat in a wide arc. Jim moved quickly to ready weapons. No way of knowing exactly what they were coming up on, but it paid to be cautious.

Adam stepped out of the enclosed cabin onto the deck, pulling his ball cap down a bit to shade his eyes, and had another look. He was always cautious—that was his nature. But the tension that rode him now as they shortened the distance between them and the other boat—well, that was new. New since that incident in the Keys. Since he'd found out how easy it was to hurt an innocent kid.

Terry sounded the siren, a signal to stop. The speaker blared. "This is the US Coast Guard. Stop your vessel. Stop your vessel."

Through the glasses, Adam could make out three figures in the boat. Instead of slowing and turning toward them, the powerboat suddenly surged away, heading toward land.

"They're making a run for it," he called.

The utility boat seemed to leap forward in response.

Jim came out, handing him a weapon, his own ready. They were closing steadily, outpowering the smaller boat. The smart thing for its occupants would be to give up the race, but if they were smuggling, they wouldn't necessarily take the smart action.

"I see weapons," Jim announced.

Adam's gut tightened. This was what they prepared for constantly. They were ready.

He braced his feet against the rush of the boat as water sprayed up on either side. Jim had his M-16 ready, waiting for the command to fire.

His nerves cranked even tighter. "Give them a warning shot."

Jim fired ahead of the boat. It didn't alter its speed.

Adam swept the boat with his glasses. They were close enough now to see faces. Three men, dark clothing, one steering, the other two armed. He moved the glasses. A tarp, covering something big enough to be almost anything. Contraband. Or people.

His heart seemed to stop for a moment. Jim was waiting for the order to fire. One of the smugglers had what looked like a rifle trained on them.

Time froze. He faced the gun, saw Jim's face turn a little toward him, waiting for the command he had to give.

But instead of the smuggler's boat, he was seeing a boat swamp, human beings spilling into the water, seeing a small body covered in blood....

He swallowed, raised his weapon. "Fire."

Before they could get off a shot, the pilot of the

other boat cut his engines. The men put their weapons at their feet, raising their hands in the air. It was over.

It was a matter of minutes to board the vessel and handcuff the smugglers. Terry was already calling it in.

Adam approached the tarp. It took everything in him to reach out and pull it back. Crates. No people, just crates.

"What d'you reckon?" Jim said. "Drugs or guns?"

"Either way, our friends here are going to have some trouble talking their way out of this one." His voice sounded almost normal.

Too bad the rest of him wasn't in such good shape. His stomach was tied up in knots, and his soul was filled with self-loathing.

He'd endangered his men. He should have given the command to fire sooner. He hadn't, because he'd been paralyzed by the past.

He'd been telling himself that he'd gotten past what happened in the Keys. He'd tamped it down so hard it only came out in nightmares.

But that wasn't getting rid of the guilt. Now it had started to affect his ability to command.

Cathy had been waiting for over a day. Adam would tell his father what she'd done. Ashton would mention it in front of Grandpa, and then...

She could picture the ensuing scene only too clearly, and she cringed at the image. She'd steeled herself all day to confront it. It hadn't happened.

She glanced at the clock on the mantel of the family room. Nearly nine. If Adam intended to come, he'd have been here by now. Still, he could have called his father.

She glanced at Ashton and Grandpa, facing each other across a checkerboard. Her tension eased. Ashton seemed totally engrossed in the game. In fact, he and Grandpa were remarkably alike in profile, and they both studied the board as intensely as if it were the instrument panel of a battleship, if battleships had such things.

For a moment the source of her comparison eluded her, and then she realized. Grandpa had served in the Navy; Ashton in the Coast Guard. But while Ashton talked easily about his service and photos of his various commands were on display in the study, Grandpa had never willingly, in all her memory, spoken of his service.

"You beat me again." Ashton didn't sound as if it bothered him much. "Never mind, I'll get you the next time."

Grandpa actually chuckled, a sound she never heard except in response to something Jamie said or did. "Set 'em up, boy, and we'll see."

"That's what my granddad used to say." Ashton's hands moved across the board. "He was a great checker player. He said it was all a matter of strategy, like any battle."

Cathy's needle froze on the pair of Jamie's shorts she was mending. Grandpa's reaction so far to the mention of his father had been a bitter tirade. Was he going to explode again?

Silence for a moment. "I'd forgot that." Grandpa's voice was gruff. "I couldn't have been more than four when he taught me to play."

She let out a relieved breath. If Grandpa's enmity toward his father had eased, that had to be good for him. Maybe learning what had happened to the woman he'd loved way back then had been healing.

Thank You, Lord. Thank You for bringing him some peace about that. Her prayer voice, silent for so long, had been stumbling back to life again since those cleansing tears she'd shed in church. Maybe she was healing, too.

"You remind me of myself when I was your age." Delia, sitting across from her, nodded at the sewing. "I always had a basket of mending overflowing. Boys are so hard on their clothes."

"To tell you the truth, I'm just happy to see him with a few rips and holes. For a long time…" She stopped, thinking of all those years when the only thing Jamie wore out was the sheets on his bed.

"He is doing well, isn't he? The way he gets around, even in those braces, is just amazing."

Jamie had been doing more lately, she realized, just since they'd been here. "Maybe the change of scenery has been good for him. He's been so excited that he's pushed himself more." She smiled. "When I put him in bed tonight, I think he was asleep before his head hit the pillow."

"My boys were like that, especially in the summer when they could be at the beach. It was like they slept just as hard as they played." Delia glanced toward the archway. "Was that the door?"

Cathy's stomach clenched. She recognized his step in the hall even before he appeared. Adam, of course. Adam, who perhaps had come to tell his father about her.

"Hey, everybody. Y'all look peaceful in here."

"I didn't expect to see you tonight, sugar." Delia rose with a swift, graceful movement and went to kiss his cheek. "How about a cup of coffee or a glass of tea? Or a piece of that peaches and cream cake your grandmother brought over?"

"Maybe later, Mama."

She patted his cheek. "I'll just go fix it. I'm sure you'll have some." She went quickly into the adjoining kitchen, not waiting for an argument.

Would he have argued? Cathy studied Adam's face as best she could without staring. He looked drawn, as if some stress roiled and bubbled under his normally pleasant façade.

Her nerves tightened. He might look that way if he anticipated a difficult family scene.

Ashton looked at his son, and she saw some sharpening of his attention, as if he saw something wrong, too.

"Jamie in bed by now, I guess?" The question was in his usual easy tone, but his right hand was fisted, pressing against his leg.

She nodded, not able to speak for the worry that clutched her throat. She should have made a clean breast of what she'd done to Ashton and Grandpa herself. Now…

The telephone rang. She heard Delia pick it up in the kitchen, heard the soft murmur of her voice. It seemed to her that the pleasant family room filled with tension. Did no one else feel it?

"Is something wrong, son?" Ashton did, obviously.

"No, sir. Well, I'd just like to have a word with you. When you've finished your game, that is."

"The game will wait." Grandpa put a checker on the board with a little click. "Go along now and have your talk."

Ashton rose. "Let's go along into the study, then. Excuse us," he added, his gaze touching Cathy.

Adam was going to tell his father. She should speak now, but her throat was tight and her mouth so dry she didn't think she could form the words. Adam followed his father from the room.

She sat, frozen.

Delia came in from the kitchen, a slip of paper in her hand, her face alight. "That was Julia on the phone," she announced. "She's set up an appointment for Jamie with a specialist. She claims he's the best orthopedist in the state, so he'll take good care of the boy." She thrust the paper at Cathy. "There's all the information about it. I declare, I'm as excited as if it were one of my boys."

Grandpa was saying something, asking something, but the blood rushing in her ears made it impossible to hear. She held in her hands the thing she'd longed for. It was literally within her grasp.

Now…well, now it could all slip away, thanks to her own actions.

Cathy couldn't seem to get her mind around everything that was happening. She walked across the quiet garden, the grass damp under her sandals. Small solar lights placed around the plantings gave a soft yellow glow to a clump of chrysanthemums here and a weeping cherry there.

She was alone, and that's what she'd desired desperately all the while Delia was explaining over again what her sister-in-law Julia had said and Grandpa was muttering his satisfaction. Just to be alone and try to figure out what was going to happen.

It was good news, yes. But her experience with

specialists had taught her that their offices expected to be paid at the time of the appointment. Was there enough in their bank account to cover a check? Maybe, barely.

And if the orthopedist recommended surgery, what then? Her hope that Grandpa had been remembered in his father's will had come to nothing. And the very fact that she'd gone looking might turn the Bodine family against her.

If Adam was even now talking to his father about it...

Miz Callie had said something to her, about how sometimes God took her life and turned it upside down. About how, when that happened, she'd had to rely only on Him.

And underneath are the everlasting arms. The scripture echoed in her mind.

Father, if You're there, if You're willing to hear me, please guide me. I don't know what to do.

"Cathy?"

She spun around at the sound of Adam's voice, her heart in her mouth.

"Mama told me about the appointment. She said you looked kind of dazed, so I came out to be sure you were all right."

She swallowed, the muscles working with an effort, as if they hadn't been used for a while. "I'm all right." The words wouldn't be held back. "Did you tell your father?"

His face seemed to tighten in the dim light. "Tell him what?" His voice was harsh.

"About what I did. Looking at the will." That had to be it. Why else would he look so severe and remote?

"No."

For a moment she thought she'd heard wrong. "But…when you wanted to talk to him alone, I was sure that was why."

His mouth compressed into a thin, hard line. In the moonlight, his face seemed stripped down to bare, uncompromising bone. "That was something else. Something private."

She drew back a little. "I wasn't meaning to pry."

"Right. I know." He shook his head. "Let's clear the air. I haven't said anything to my father about your excursion to the courthouse. I won't."

"Thank you." Something was wrong. She could sense it. Something boiled away under the surface, but whatever it was, he wasn't going to tell her.

"About the appointment—you are going to take Jamie, aren't you?"

She turned away a little, not sure she wanted that laserlike gaze on her face. "I don't know."

"Why not?" he demanded. "It's what you wanted, isn't it?"

"Of course it's what I want. But is it fair to get Jamie's hopes up? I don't want to make him think he's going to be able to walk and run if there's no way to make that happen."

"At least you have to see what the doctor says. We can cross the next bridge when we come to it."

"We? This is a decision for me to make, no one else."

He caught her arm, turning her around to face him. "You have to do what's best for Jamie, even if that means letting me help."

Her anger sparked suddenly, and she was glad, because otherwise she had a feeling she might burst into tears.

"I always do what's best for Jamie. You don't even like me, so don't say you're including yourself out of friendship. You just pity my son."

"You haven't let me get close enough to know whether I like you or not." He was angry enough that it broke through his habitual calm, and he seemed glad of it as well. "But I care for Jamie, and like it or not, you're family."

Her lips twisted. "Grandpa is family. You heard him. I'm just a stepgranddaughter who's no real kin at all."

He grasped both her arms, holding her firmly. If he had an urge to shake her, he suppressed it.

"Kin or not, Jamie is a hurting kid who needs help. I'm not going to let anything stand in the way of his getting it. So you and Jamie are keeping that appointment, and I'm going with you."

"No." Everything in her rebelled at that thought. "I've taken Jamie to plenty of doctor's visits on my own. I don't need any company."

"Well, this time you're not going to be alone." It was said with an implacable finality.

"Why?" she demanded. "Why do you want to?"

He stared at her for a long moment, his face so close that even in the feeble light she could see every line. Then he lowered his head and kissed her.

It wasn't like the first time. That had been almost tentative, taking them both by surprise.

This was surer, with a determination that took her breath away and had her clinging to his strong arms.

He drew back, letting her go so quickly that she nearly lost her balance. "I don't know what's going on between us, but there's something." He sounded almost angry about it. "We're connected, even if it's something neither of us wants. So I'm doing this one thing for you and Jamie, like it or not."

He turned and walked away. She couldn't have called after him if she wanted to, because she had no words to say.

She put her hand to her lips, as if to wipe off his kiss, and touched them lightly instead. Even if it's something neither of us wants, he'd said. Well, that made his feelings clear, at any rate.

And hers, too, she assured herself. She didn't want a relationship with anyone, and certainly not with Adam. The complications of that made her head reel.

But one thing, at least, she couldn't deny. She couldn't go back to being the woman she'd been the day they'd met, safe and untouchable as a turtle inside its shell.

From here on out, she'd changed, because now she knew she was vulnerable to love.

Chapter Nine

"I just wish y'all were staying out at the beach house with me." Miz Callie snipped off a deep rust mum and admired it before putting it in the basket on her arm. "Not that Delia and Ashton aren't delighted to have you, but you couldn't help loving being right there at the beach."

"I'm sure we would, but Grandpa seems to have his mind set." Cathy cut a handful of marigolds, inhaling the spicy scent.

"That's one stubborn man." Miz Callie gave her a pixielike smile that made the older woman look about six. "All the Bodine men are. They need careful handling."

She gave an inward shudder. "Believe me, managing Grandpa is a tough task, even when it's for his own good."

"I wonder how many of these flowers Delia wants

to take to the nursing home." Miz Callie surveyed the basket. "Maybe a few more, anyway."

Cathy nodded, bending to the clipping. It was ridiculous, the way she was beginning to feel about this garden. At least if they were at the beach house, she wouldn't have to be constantly reminded of kissing Adam.

Miz Callie touched her hand. "Not that one. It's past its prime."

Cathy looked down, to see that she'd been about to cut a faded flower head. "Sorry. I wasn't concentrating."

Miz Callie clasped her hand. "If you want to talk about the thing that's upsetting you, I'd be glad to listen."

For a crazy moment she thought Miz Callie knew about Adam—about what they'd said, about that kiss. But Miz Callie was talking about the appointment for Jamie. She had to be.

"I'm not upset exactly about seeing the specialist. It's just that Jamie's been through so much, and now, thinking about it all again…"

"I know. But it is for the best, isn't it?" Miz Callie's tone was warm, inviting confidences.

Cathy nodded. "You know, you said something to me that I've been thinking about a lot. About how sometimes God turns your life upset down, and all you have to cling to is Him."

"That's what it's like for you here, isn't it?

Finding out you have a whole mess of family you never knew about, and coming here, taking your grandfather and your son out of their familiar environment. I know how upsetting that can be. No matter what it's like, sometimes we just long for home."

"We don't exactly live like this, that's for sure." She smiled, nodding at the gracious old house.

"Things have been hard for you financially." Miz Callie seemed to approach the subject delicately.

"I guess you'd say that, but it was familiar. Safe." Hard and frugal as life had been for the past few years, she'd felt safe in a way she didn't now.

"Safe, yes. I can see that. Ned's been hiding from the past for a long time, clinging to his anger to keep him safe from feeling hurt."

She couldn't argue. That was exactly what Grandpa had been doing; she knew that now.

"Well." Miz Callie's tone turned brisk. "Ned took a good first step in coming here. He's even stopped correcting me when I call him Ned. Now the next thing is to get him to go to the beach house, where all the trouble took place. Will you help me persuade him?"

"I…I don't know. He'll be angry."

Miz Callie straightened, looking into Cathy's eyes. "Why does that bother you so much, sugar? It's not the end of the world if he gets mad."

"I didn't mean…" She had to stop and start over,

because she surely wasn't making herself very clear, and Miz Callie's firm gaze didn't allow for evasions.

"We owe him a great deal, Jamie and I. If he hadn't taken us in, I don't know what would have become of us."

Her mind winced away from the memories of that terrible time. If Grandpa hadn't come to the rescue, what would have happened? She could have ended up in jail, like as not, and Jamie in foster care.

"Well, of course he took you in. You're his grand-daughter. He loves you. And I know you love him." Miz Callie hesitated for a moment. "All right. I see it distresses you, so I won't ask for your help. I'll just tackle Ned myself and persuade him."

"No." Cathy found her voice suddenly. Hadn't she just told herself she couldn't keep trying to play it safe? "I'll help you."

Adam ran down the beach near the house he shared with three friends on Isle of Palms. Was he trying to run away from the issues that dogged him? If so, it wasn't working. They pounded in his head in rhythm with the pounding of his feet.

He'd been so sure he was over the events of that terrible day off the Keys. In the initial aftermath, he'd had a few bad weeks. That was only natural— the whole crew had.

But they'd done their duty anyway. They'd moved on. It was all part of the job.

But now Jamie had somehow triggered the memories. The guilt. And it had come back in a way that might have jeopardized his crew. If he was going to second-guess his every command, he was no good to anyone.

Neither Terry nor Jim had said anything. They wouldn't. But that didn't mean they weren't doubting him.

He'd intended to talk to his father about it the night before last, but it hadn't worked out the way he planned. Once they were alone, he couldn't seem to say it, flat out.

I think I'm losing my grip as an officer.

Instead he'd talked all around it, leaving Daddy none the wiser. He slowed to a jog as he started up the path through the dunes.

His father had tried to be supportive. He'd expressed confidence in Adam, which just made him feel worse.

And then there was Cathy. He really didn't want to go there, even in his thoughts. He'd made about every possible mistake he could make where she was concerned.

He slowed to a walk as he approached the deck. His cousin Hugh sat in one of the deck chairs, making himself comfortable, a can of soda in his hand, which he raised in greeting.

Adam dropped into the chair next to him. "Raiding our fridge already, I see."

"Your roommate offered. He was on his way out."

"Not that you wouldn't have helped yourself anyway. What's wrong? No classes to teach on the niceties of maritime law today?"

"Not until ten. What about you? You off-duty today?"

He nodded, leaning his head against the back of the chair and closing his eyes against the sun. "I'm supposed to pick up Uncle Ned and the others later to take them to Miz Callie's. She and Cathy finally convinced him to visit the beach house."

He felt himself frowning and tried to eliminate the expression. Hugh would be on to that like a shot. When Miz Callie asked Adam to bring them, she'd talked about how reluctant Cathy had been to face making her grandfather angry.

Something isn't right between them, Miz Callie had said. *It's something to do with why she came to live with him, and whatever it is, it's grieving her. You should talk to her, Adam.*

No, he shouldn't. Things got out of control whenever he tried to talk to Cathy.

"So, anything new with Cathy Norwood?" Hugh asked the question casually, but there was something behind it not so casual.

"No." Not exactly. Not unless you counted kissing her, along with a few other disturbing things.

Hugh didn't buy that. He could tell without looking.

"I found something," Hugh said. "Don't know how significant it is, but it is there."

Adam straightened, swinging to face him. "What?"

"A few years back, in an Atlanta suburb, Cathleen Norwood was arrested for robbing a pharmacy."

"Drugs?" His mind leapt to the obvious conclusion.

"I don't know that. The record was too vague to tell." Hugh's tone suggested that any records he kept about a case would be in pristine order. "I'm still trying to find out more."

Everything in him denied the possibility. "Are you sure it's the same Cathleen Norwood?"

Hugh nodded. "They faxed me the photo. It's her, all right."

His stomach did an uncomfortable twist. It couldn't be. But apparently it was. "There has to be more info than that."

"No details, no record of the disposition of the case. I'm working on it. Someone has to know something."

"Maybe that means the charges were dismissed." He was grasping at straws, and he knew it.

"Maybe. I'm staying on it." Hugh gave him a

level look. "Seems like you ought to tell me whatever else it is that's bugging you."

He'd told Cathy he wouldn't tell his father about the business of the will. He hadn't said anything about Hugh. That was a rationalization, and he knew it.

But he had to tell Hugh. "Somethin' happened the other day that—well, it doesn't have to mean anything. But my daddy dropped Cathy downtown because he thought she wanted to walk around the historic district. Turned out she had something else in mind. She went to the courthouse and looked up the terms of our great-grandfather's will."

Hugh let out a low whistle. "She wanted to see if her grandfather was mentioned. Is he?"

"No. The existing will was written in 1950, after Great-Grandfather's wife died, when he probably thought Ned was dead, too. Maybe Ned had been mentioned in an earlier one. Bound to be, I'd think, but that doesn't make a difference in law. And Cathy looking it up doesn't have to mean anything."

"What did she say when you confronted her about it?"

He shrugged. "What you'd expect. That she was looking out for her grandfather. That they had a right to know. Which is true, as far as it goes."

"But you don't like the idea that she kept it quiet, and neither do I." Hugh finished the thought for him.

Adam blew out an exasperated breath. "It doesn't have to mean anything. Even if she was arrested once…" He let that thought die off, because it didn't lead anywhere good.

"We don't have to tell anyone else what we've found out, but we can't leave it alone. If she's trying to run some kind of scam on Miz Callie, we have to know." Hugh rose, one hand on the chair arm. "You don't like this. Neither do I. But we'll do what we have to do to protect Miz Callie."

No matter who got hurt. He saw Jamie's face in his mind, felt the soft warmth of Cathy's lips. He knew, only too well, who could get hurt.

He stood, facing his cousin. "You find out what you can about that business in Atlanta. I'll keep tabs on Cathy, especially when she's around Miz Callie." He hated this, but Hugh was right. They didn't have a choice.

Cathy tried to lean back and relax as Adam's car crossed the bridge to Sullivan's Island. *Please, Lord, let this visit to his old home go well for my grandfather today.*

After all her apprehension about bringing up the subject of going to the island house, she and Miz Callie hadn't had to try very hard to persuade him. She'd had a growing sense, through his reaction, that perhaps he was ready to make peace with the past.

Oh, he'd put up a token resistance, but he hadn't been angry. He'd finally said she and Miz Callie were a matched set, so convinced they knew what was best for him.

That had pleased her, being compared to Miz Callie. She admired the woman more every time they met. It would be nice to think she could grow into the kind of strong but serene Christian woman Miz Callie was.

Next to her in the backseat, Jamie could hardly contain his excitement at going to the beach again. Apparently whatever lingering fear he might have felt after his ducking was gone for good. And Lindsay had promised to come and play as soon as she got home from school, which was the icing on the cake for him.

"I expect a couple of those restaurants are new since your day," Adam commented, waving his hand toward the small wooden buildings that clustered near the island's main intersection.

Grandpa leaned forward in his seat, and she thought she saw a little excitement in the way he moved, like Jamie when he spotted something. "There was a store on that corner," he said. "And the firehouse was right down here a ways."

"Still there," Adam said with the air of someone on familiar ground. "There's a park adjacent to it now."

"Look at that. I remember when I used to ride

my bicycle down here, before I could drive. We'd stop down at the store and get penny candy in a little paper bag." He leaned back to address Jamie over his shoulder. "You'd like that, Jamie."

"I wish I could ride a bike."

Grandpa had meant the candy, of course, but Jamie focused on the thing he'd rather have. Her gaze met Adam's in the rearview mirror, and a jolt of awareness went through her.

"Maybe you will, one day," she said, patting Jamie's leg. *Please, God.*

After such a long dry spell, she seemed to be praying almost as much as talking. If only she could be sure her prayers were heard….

Adam turned off the main road toward the ocean, and she could almost feel Grandpa's tension level mount.

"Lots of fancy new houses out here now," he said.

"I know this was all different during the war years," Adam said. "Miz Callie says the military took over much of the ocean side of the island."

Grandpa nodded. He stared at the new beach houses, but she didn't think he was seeing them. "Gun batteries up from Fort Moultrie at this end, and down by Breech Inlet at the other. We were ready for an invasion, y'see."

It was hard to equate that with the peaceful

vacation playground the island was now. "I never thought of it as a military installation," she said.

"Had to be." Grandpa's voice roughened. "German subs were going up and down the coast. We had to be ready." His hand gripped the armrest tightly.

The car slowed, and then they were pulling up at the beach house. Even as Adam parked the car, Miz Callie came scurrying down the stairs to meet them, her face alight with smiles.

"My goodness, I'm so happy to see you." She had Grandpa's door open in an instant. "Come in, come in. Sorry there's so many steps, but I guess you remember that."

Grandpa got out slowly, as if reluctance was setting in. Miz Callie didn't give him time to think about it, though. She took his arm, leading him up the steps, with Adam steadying him on the other side.

Cathy bent to pick up Jamie, but he pushed her hands away.

"I can go up by myself, Mama."

She drew back at the firmness in his tone. "Are you sure, sugar? There are a lot of steps."

"I can do it."

Let him do things for himself, the doctor had said. It wasn't easy, but she tried to obey. She stood back. His small face intent, Jamie grabbed the railing and started up behind Adam.

Was this because Adam was there? She knew how much her son looked up to him. Her heart winced at the thought. She couldn't let Jamie be hurt by that innocent admiration. Given Adam's complex attitude toward her, the chances of that probably increased every day.

Occupied with this fresh worry over Jamie, she hardly noticed how Grandpa was doing until they were all inside. He stood for a moment, looking at the long, welcoming room. It was slightly shabby with its well-worn furniture and shelves full of books, but everything in it seemed to reach out harmoniously to pull you in.

"It's changed from what you remember, I suppose." Miz Callie grasped Grandpa's arm and led him to a padded rocking chair. "We replaced some pieces of furniture over the years."

Grandpa didn't respond. Instead, he seemed concentrated on turning the rocking chair so it faced into the room. She could see the tightness of his jaw, the way his hands trembled as he adjusted the chair, and her apprehension rose.

Please don't let this be a mistake.

"I remember when Richmond and I were young marrieds." Miz Callie settled in a chair next to him. "Those three boys of ours used to drive us crazy to get out here every summer."

Grandpa seemed to rouse himself. "Y'all came through Hurricane Hugo all right?"

"Some damage, but not as bad as we thought when we first saw the place. We were in the city when Hugo hit, and it was days before they were going to let us back on. So Richmond took his boat and slipped past, just so we'd know the house was still standing, at least."

Jamie, apparently getting bored with the grown-up talk, tugged at her hand. "Mama, please may I go to the beach? Please?"

She glanced at her grandfather, not sure she wanted to leave him alone at what surely must be an emotional time for him.

"I'll take Jamie down," Adam said. "We'll just play on the beach," he added, a reminder of her anger the day he'd taken Jamie in the surf.

She glanced from Jamie's pleading blue eyes to Adam's level gaze. "All right. Thank you. Jamie, you listen to Cousin Adam, mind."

It was probably an unnecessary injunction. Jamie admired Adam too much to disobey.

The two of them headed out the sliding glass door to the deck hand in hand. Jamie was chattering at Adam as they disappeared from view.

She sat down, trying to concentrate on her grandfather and Miz Callie. Miz Callie was doing most of the talking, but it did seem as if Grandpa's tension was easing. His hand, clasping the arm of the rocker, gradually relaxed.

Miz Callie had a gift for putting people at ease.

Her gentle flow of conversation streamed past, mentioning people who were probably long dead, recalling picnics on the beach and long-ago storms that brought strange driftwood floating ashore.

She couldn't hear Jamie's voice any longer. Moving across to the sliding glass door, she put her hand on the frame, but she couldn't see the beach from this angle, just a dizzying expanse of ocean and sky.

"Go on out and see what they're doing," Grandpa said. "You know you're never satisfied when someone else is watching the boy."

That jolted her. It was true, but she hadn't realized she was being that obvious.

"Why don't we all go out on the deck where we can see them?" Miz Callie rose with one of her quick movements and seized Grandpa's arm. "Come along, Ned. We'll sit outside for a bit."

Propelled by her enthusiasm, he rose, shoving himself up with his hands, muttering something Cathy didn't catch. She pushed the sliding door open and stepped out onto the deck, hearing Jamie's voice over the gentle murmur of the surf. There they were, digging in the sand—

"Ned!"

Cathy whirled at the panic in Miz Callie's voice, but not quite in time. Grandpa had turned, halfway through the door, twisting his body. With a muffled gasp, he fell, hitting the floor heavily, ominously still.

Chapter Ten

"Is Jamie asleep?" Miz Callie gave Cathy a concerned look as she came out onto the deck at the beach house.

"Yes, finally." Cathy sank into the chair next to her, feeling as if she'd been pulled through a knothole backward. "I checked on Grandpa, and he's sound asleep, too. Whatever the doctor gave him must have knocked him out."

"At least the worst of it seems to be the wrenched knee." Miz Callie poured iced tea from a pitcher on the table between them into a waiting glass. "This is herbal, so it won't keep you awake."

"I don't think anything could keep me awake tonight." She held the glass against her throbbing temples. "What a day. If you and Adam hadn't been here when Grandpa fell…"

"Mostly Adam," Miz Callie said quickly. "I declare, that boy was born to command. I've never seen anything like how he can stay calm and take control in a difficult situation."

She nodded. Funny, but she hadn't thought much about Adam in his role as a military officer until those frightening moments this afternoon. He'd run up the steps carrying Jamie in what seemed like seconds after Miz Callie shouted for him.

He'd persuaded Grandpa to stay still until the paramedics had checked him out, something Grandpa certainly wouldn't have done for her. And while he refused to go to the hospital, Adam had gotten his agreement to let Miz Callie's physician neighbor, who'd come running at the sight of the paramedics' van, look him over as well.

"He certainly handled my grandfather better than I could. Grandpa hates to depend on me when it's something to do with his health. I'm just praying it's not anything more serious than his knee."

"Ben Phillips is a good doctor. I'm sure when he saw the paramedics, he thought it was me." Miz Callie chuckled a little at the idea. "But if he'd suspected anything worse, he'd have gotten Ned to the hospital one way or another."

"I know Grandpa insisted he was all right, but I could tell he was shaken." That had been one of the scariest moments in her life until she'd reached him and found he was still breathing.

"Men never want to admit there's anything wrong with them," Miz Callie said. "His brother was just like him. When Richmond had his first stroke, I was at my wits' end trying to get him to do what the doctor said. At least Ned is following orders tonight."

The doctor had urged them not to try and go back to the house in Mount Pleasant tonight, insisting that Grandpa was better off to go straight to bed. He was supposed to stay off his knee for a few days, at least.

"Maybe now that Ned's here, he'll be willing to stay even longer." Miz Callie's brow furrowed. "That fall of his—did you see how it happened?"

Cathy shook her head. "I was looking out at the beach when I heard you exclaim. Why? Didn't he just lose his balance? He does sometimes have dizzy spells."

"Maybe." Miz Callie sounded doubtful. "But it seemed to me that something happened when he looked out there." She waved a hand toward the ocean, a dark moving mass beyond the pale strip of sand in the dim light. "He got a look almost of panic in his face, and he jerked around, like he was going back inside. That's when he fell. Has he ever said anything that would make you think he feared the water?"

"No, but living where we did, it never came up."

"It's a bit of a mystery. Maybe he'll talk about it tomorrow."

"Maybe." But she doubted it. Grandpa wasn't one to talk about his feelings. "What if I was wrong to urge him to come?" She didn't realize until she said the words that it had been troubling her.

"Surely it was the natural thing to do, once Adam found him. Wasn't it?"

"I guess so. But I didn't really think it through at the time. I wanted him to reconcile with his family, but…" Cathy let that trail off, afraid she was about to say more to Miz Callie than she wanted.

"Maybe you really wanted family to help you bear the burden." Miz Callie reached across to clasp her hand. "There's nothing wrong with that, child."

She shook her head. "He's my responsibility, just as Jamie is. But I jumped at the chance to come here because…well, because it seemed as if we were stuck in a situation we couldn't get out of. At least coming here was a change."

"You felt that way because you were trying to do it all alone," Miz Callie insisted. "There's nothing wrong with leaning on family."

She took a shaky breath. "I should have considered that if he'd stayed away all these years, there had to be a reason. What if he really can't deal with the past? Maybe it's wrong to try and force it."

"If that's true, then I'm equally to blame. I pushed it, even knowing that Ned must not want to be found." Miz Callie patted her hand. "So if we're wrong, we're wrong for the best of reasons."

"I'm not sure my reasons were all that pure."

"You had hopes of something good happening for Jamie here," Miz Callie said.

She couldn't... "How do you know that?"

"Because if I were in your place, that's what I'd have been hoping, too. There's no need to be upset about it, Cathy. You and Adam will take Jamie to the specialist, and maybe the man will have good news for you."

So she knew about Adam going along to the doctor. What else did she know? She couldn't know what Cathy's feelings were, because she didn't know herself.

"I've told Adam that he doesn't have to go with us to the appointment. I can manage."

"Nonsense." Miz Callie was brisk. "We won't let you go into that alone, and as attached as Jamie is to Adam, it'll be good for the boy to have him there."

"Jamie is getting attached to him." She twined her fingers together, wishing she could see her way clearly. "Maybe too much so. When...when we go back home, and Jamie doesn't see Adam anymore, he'll be devastated."

"Surely a child can't have too many people loving him, whatever happens." Miz Callie patted her hand again, and it seemed to Cathy that love flowed through the woman's touch. "As for the rest… Well, let's just wait and see what tomorrow brings. One thing I do know, and that's that God is working in this situation. We just have to have faith."

Cathy nodded. She was trying, but her belief in happy endings had vanished a long time ago.

The warm water of the tidal pool washed over Cathy's feet and legs, soothing her. After a difficult night, in which she'd wakened a half-dozen times in the strange bed, listening for Grandpa or Jamie, the combination of sunlight and warm ocean water relaxed her to the point of mindlessness. The beach was deserted this afternoon, the only sound the soft, constant murmur of the surf and the cry of a gull.

She was dawdling, putting off the moment at which she had to tell Jamie about his appointment with the doctor tomorrow. She didn't have much hope that he'd be happy about it. Having his vacation interrupted by one of his least favorite things was sure to lead to tears. He might, at some level, understand that it was for his own good, but that didn't mean he'd like it.

Jamie, delighted to be free of his braces, floated in the warm, shallow water of the tidal pool. Floating was a new accomplishment, and he practiced it endlessly.

A small parade of sandpipers, put off guard by their stillness, trailed close to Jamie. He popped up when he saw them, and they veered off, still in formation, like a school of fish.

"Look at the sandpipers, Mama. Why do they all walk together like that?"

"I don't know, sugar." Just one of the things she didn't know about this new environment of theirs.

"I'll ask Adam. He'll know." Jamie was confident that his hero knew everything.

Be careful, sugar. Don't get too close. You might get hurt.

She couldn't say that, but she wanted to. "I'm sure he knows," she said instead. "Are you getting cold?"

"No, ma'am," he said instantly, lying back in the water again. "It feels good. I love it here, don't you, Mama? I want to stay here always."

Her heart seemed to contract. It was natural he'd say that, wasn't it? Any child might express a wish to stay at the seashore forever.

"I like it here, too. But if we stayed forever, we'd start to miss our house, and the garden, and the mountains."

"Not me," he said instantly. "I like the ocean better."

Trying to persuade him otherwise would be a

waste of time, and it wasn't accomplishing the task of preparing him for the doctor's visit.

"Jamie, I wanted to tell you—"

"Look, Mama, there's Cousin Adam!" Jamie sat up, sending ripples splashing over her legs. "Adam! We're here, Adam!" He shouted before she could stop him, waving frantically at the tall figure on the deck.

Not that stopping him would have done any good anyway. Adam was clearly intent on joining them, trotting down the steps and starting down the path.

In a moment, it seemed, he was walking across the sand toward them, pausing only to ditch the mocs he wore with shorts and a T-shirt. He stopped next to her, and all of a sudden she couldn't seem to breathe.

She would not look up at him. She couldn't let him see how he affected her.

"Hey. You two look nice and comfortable. I saw you floating, buddy. You're doin' great."

Jamie "swam" over to him, his hands touching the sandy bottom of the pool. "I like to float. I want to swim next."

"You're getting there." Adam sat down next to her, putting his feet in the water. "Floating comes first. Pretty soon you'll be swimming like a fish. Or like your cousin Win. He swims even better than a fish."

"Now," Jamie said instantly. "Teach me now, Adam."

"I don't think so." Cathy managed a distant smile for Adam. "We were about ready to go up."

"Not already," Jamie wailed.

"Not already," Adam echoed. His smile had an edge to it, as if he knew she wanted to cut short their time together.

It cut into her, that mocking smile. Impossible as it was, she wanted to see a wholehearted smile from him, one that said that everything was good between them.

It wasn't going to happen. Even when he'd kissed her, he'd been quick to point out the barriers between them.

Maybe she could convince herself she felt nothing if he weren't sitting next to her, so close she could feel the heat radiating from his skin.

"I…I need to talk to Jamie about something," she said, hoping he'd take the hint.

"Go ahead," he said. "Don't let me stop you." He leaned back lazily on his hands, but there was a glint in his eyes that challenged her.

"What, Mama?" Naturally Jamie followed the conversation she didn't want him to.

She leaned forward to touch his wet cheek, trying to ignore Adam. Useless.

"I just wanted to tell you that tomorrow morning we're going to see a new doctor, right here in Charleston. He's going to check you out."

Jamie's face clouded instantly. "I don't wanna see any old doctor. Anyway, Lindsay's coming tomorrow, so I can't."

"Lindsay isn't coming until she gets home from school. We'll be back long before that, I promise."

His lower lip came out. "I still don't want to. He'll make me move my legs and he'll poke me and it'll hurt."

That was such a true assessment that she couldn't speak for a moment. It would hurt. Was she right to put him through more pain when she couldn't promise it would lead to anything good?

"Listen, Jamie." Adam slid down into the water next to Jamie, apparently not bothered by dousing his shorts and shirt. He pulled Jamie over to him. "I'm going to go with you and your mama tomorrow, okay? I know it's not fun to be poked and prodded, but sometimes we have to. And I'll be right there with you, I promise."

Jamie gave him a look that would have melted her heart if it were turned on her. "Do I have to?"

Adam nodded. "It's your duty."

"Oh." Jamie pondered that for a moment. "I guess I have to." He gripped Adam's wet arm. "You promise you'll be there?"

"I promise." Adam said the words as if they were an oath.

"Okay, then."

Cathy took a shaky breath, not sure whether to smile or cry. Adam had gotten past Jamie's resistance to the doctor visit better than she could have. But he'd done it at the cost of reminding her just how much Jamie would be hurt if the day came when Adam made a promise he didn't keep.

Aware of Adam's gaze on her face, she turned away, reaching for the towels. "Come on, sugar. We really do have to go up. Miz Callie is fixing supper for us, and I heard her say there's going to be fried chicken."

"I love fried chicken."

Adam lifted him, dripping, from the water. "Reckon we'd best get up there, then."

Jamie rode on Adam's back up to the house, pelting him with questions about the sandpipers. She followed, wrestling with her feelings.

"I want to go up the steps all by myself," Jamie demanded when they reached the bottom of the wooden stairs.

Adam swung him down and deposited him next to the railing. "There you go, buddy."

His face intent, Jamie grasped the railing and started up. When Adam moved to go behind him, she put her hand on his arm to stop him.

His skin was sun-warmed to her touch, and when

he looked down at her, she forgot for an instant what she intended to say.

"Thank you. For helping reconcile him to going to the doctor. He hates it so, and I..." She stopped, not sure she wanted to say any more to him about it.

"You're worrying that it's wrong to put him through it with no guarantees."

"How did you know that?"

He shrugged. "It's natural enough."

"Maybe it's natural because it's right." She wasn't used to doubting and questioning her course of action so much. She didn't like it.

He put his hand over hers. "We all have to do things that are unpleasant sometimes. You can't protect Jamie from that."

"But—"

"Adam, are you comin'?" Jamie, halfway up, turned to look at them.

"Right now," Adam said. He took the steps two at a time to catch up, Jamie giggling at him.

Her heart turned over. Seeing Jamie healthy and happy was all she wanted. But the more he...the more they...depended on Adam, the greater the hurt was going to be in the end.

Adam checked his watch again. They'd been waiting in the exam room for ten minutes. Despite the colorful Noah's Ark painting on the walls and the box of toys in the corner, Jamie had become increasingly restless.

Adam could hardly blame the kid. He wasn't too fond of waiting around for unpleasant things, either. Just get on with it and get it over with—that was his motto.

He focused on Cathy's face. She was trying to interest Jamie in a toy from the box, but he could read the tension in her every movement.

Ever since Hugh had told him about the arrest record, his thoughts about Cathy had been in flux. The cynical part of his mind insisted that he was here to make sure that the possible treatment for Jamie's condition wasn't being used to scam the family. But his heart told him he was there to support Jamie any way he could.

No doubt about it, Hugh's revelation had poisoned the way he looked at Cathy. Just when he thought he had her sized up, something came out of the woodwork to upset his picture of her.

Jamie, having rejected every toy in the box, came to lean against Adam's knee. "What's this for?" He touched the insignia on Adam's uniform.

Since he'd come in the middle of the day, he wore his utility uniform, dark blue pants and shirt, dark blue ball cap.

"That shows what service I belong to." He plopped his cap on Jamie's head, where it slid down to his ears. "Coasties wear dark blue ball caps with their insignia on the front." He took Jamie's finger and traced the gold lettering. "See, when your great-grandpa was in the Navy, he wore a round white cap—what they call a dixie-cup hat."

"I didn't know that." Jamie leaned closer, fidgeting a bit. "I wish that doctor would come."

Adam put his arm around the small shoulders. "I wish that, too. Waiting is hard."

"Yeah. I'm glad you're here." He rested his head against Adam's shoulder.

He might just as well have reached into his chest and squeezed Adam's heart. "You know, sometimes at work my team has to wait and wait. We're waiting for the SAR alarm to go off."

"What's SAR?"

You could always count on Jamie's curiosity. "That stands for search and rescue. It means someone is in trouble out on the ocean, and we have to go out and help them."

"Is it scary?"

"Sometimes." When the waves were higher than buildings. When the wind howled so you couldn't hear anything else, and the water was cold enough to freeze your bones. The unofficial Coast Guard motto was only too apt. *You have to go out, but you don't have to come back.* "But I'd still rather be doing that than anything else."

"Why?"

He'd just thought to distract the boy, not get into

such deep waters. But the answer wasn't really that hard. It was the answer most Coasties would give.

"I get to help people. Sometimes even save their lives. There's nothing better than that."

The door opened, and he could feel Cathy's nerves jump through the six feet of space that separated them.

"Hello there." Compact and graying, the man had the look of somebody who spent time on the water—bright eyes, a ruddy color in his cheeks, creases of sun lines in his skin. "You must be Jamie. I'm Dr. McMillan."

He held out his hand to Jamie first, which seemed to awe the boy. At a nudge from Adam, he shook hands solemnly.

"Mrs. Norwood." He turned to Cathy. "You'll have to forgive my double take. I didn't realize your husband is in the Coast Guard. I'm surprised you're not at a military hospital."

Color rushed into Cathy's cheeks. Before she could speak, Adam did.

"I'm just a relative, doc. Here to keep Jamie company."

"I see. Well, that's fine." Dr. McMillan hooked a stool with the toe of his shoe and rolled it over to sit down, a fat folder in his hands. "I think I have all of Jamie's records here, and I've gone over them carefully. I would suggest that after my exam today, you bring him in for a complete new set of X-rays. I can see this young man has been growing since his last ones."

Jamie straightened, as if determined to be as tall as he could.

"So." He smiled at Jamie. "Let's get the exam over with, shall we?"

For an instant, Jamie clung to Adam's hand. Then he gave a small nod and stepped toward the doctor, shoulders back, head erect.

"Good man," McMillan said.

The next few minutes weren't easy, even for Adam. Obviously the doctor had to understand Jamie's range of motion. Just as obviously, the exam hurt the boy.

Cathy was strong and encouraging, her voice even, but her face was white, and every little murmur from Jamie deepened the pain in her eyes.

Finally, after what seemed an endless time but was probably not more than five minutes, the doctor helped Jamie put his shirt back on.

"Good job, Jamie. I can tell you're a military man, just like your…" He paused, nodding to Adam.

"My cousin Adam," Jamie said. "He's in the Coast Guard. He saves people's lives."

"We have a lot in common," the doctor said. "Now I'm going to let Nurse Penny take you out to the playroom while I talk to your mother and Cousin Adam for a minute, okay?"

Somewhat to Adam's surprise, Jamie nodded, going off willingly with the smiling nurse. When he'd gone, Dr. McMillan turned to Cathy.

"We'll want to have a careful study of the X-rays, of course, but based on what I'm seeing, Jamie has had fine results from his earlier surgeries. As far as the hip defect is concerned, I think we can be confident that a single surgery will correct that entirely."

Cathy didn't move. Tears welled in her eyes and spilled over onto her cheeks, and she didn't even seem to realize it. "You're sure?" Her voice was choked.

"Nothing's one hundred percent guaranteed," the doctor said. "But I've seen enough cases like Jamie's to be quite confident." He patted her shoulder. "I know. It's been a long, hard struggle since he was born, but the end is in sight now." He rose, moving toward the door, his briskness returning. "You'll fix up the X-rays with my nurse, and she'll call you with a date for the surgery."

Then he was gone, the door swinging shut behind him.

Cathy stood, and he rose with her, not sure what to do or say. She stared at him like someone blind.

"Cathy?" He took her hand, almost afraid to

touch her. "It's good news. Jamie is going to be fine. You heard the doctor. Don't lose heart now."

"I'm not. I…" She seemed to lose whatever she wanted to say, her face crumpling.

In an instant had her in his arms. Patting her shoulder, murmuring comforting words. "It's all right. It's going to be all right."

First Jamie, now Cathy, squeezing his heart until he could barely breathe. He brushed his cheek against the softness of her hair, feeling her pain for her son, her grief for what he'd endured, her overwhelming emotion at the prospect of a future for him.

This much, at least, of Cathy was true. Whatever else she was hiding, this was real.

He held her close, knowing he was long past warning himself not to get involved with her. He cared. This wasn't random attraction. This was caring, and he suspected it would end up hurting both of them.

Chapter Eleven

Cathy picked at the French fries on the tray in front of her, her throat still too tight to enjoy eating. Adam had insisted that Jamie pick a place to stop for lunch on the way back from the doctor's office. Jamie's taste, like that of most six-year-olds, ran to fast-food hamburgers with a prize in the bag, a treat he seldom had.

Since it was past lunchtime, the restaurant was nearly empty. Jamie, with his resilient good spirits, had bolted his sandwich and gone into the play area, where he was engrossed in crawling through the plastic tunnel.

She watched him, feeling her tension easing. He was enjoying himself. He didn't understand the ramifications of what had happened today.

Adam came back to the table, carrying refills on their iced teas.

"Here you go. Not as good as homemade, but at

least it's wet and cold." His gaze scanned her face. "Better now?"

She felt the heat mounting in her cheeks. How could she have broken down the way she had in front of him? Did she have no pride? She had to put some barriers back between them.

"Yes. Thank you," she added. "I'm fine."

"The doctor's report is good news," he said, as if she'd questioned that.

She rubbed her temples, nodding. Of course it was good news that the specialist thought surgery would work, if she could find a way to make it happen.

"I...I'll have to talk with Dr. McMillan about the surgery." She swallowed, throat muscles working. "About what the fees will be. Maybe he'd let us pay him a little at a time."

Adam didn't respond for a moment—long enough for her to wish she hadn't said that. She didn't want to discuss her finances with him, especially after the fiasco over her looking at the will.

"That might be more likely if you had a job," Adam said.

For an instant she could only stare at him. Then anger came to her aid. Was that really what he thought of her—that she was a freeloader?

"A job?" Her voice rose despite her effort at control. "I have two, as a matter of fact. I work part-time at the truck stop, waiting tables. And I also clean houses for people."

"I didn't know—" he began.

"Maybe cleaning houses isn't much of a job by your standards, but I have to do something that I can fit around taking care of Grandpa and Jamie. I didn't finish college, so I can't get something that pays enough for the kind of care they need. I've tried working full-time, and each time, either Jamie hits a bad spell or Grandpa does, and I have to quit."

"Cathy, I didn't realize. I mean, you never mentioned working."

"No, you didn't realize." The lump was back in her throat, and her anger drained away, leaving her exhausted. "How could somebody like you, like any member of your family, understand wondering how you're going to buy groceries or pay for medicine for a sick child? You've never had to think twice about it."

"I guess I can't understand."

Was that doubt in his voice? Maybe he didn't believe her. Maybe he thought she was trying to con him. Right now she was too wiped out to care. She was tired of struggling and overwhelmed at the thought of having Jamie's wholeness within reach and maybe losing it. She couldn't sit here and defend herself to him any longer.

"We'd better go," she said abruptly. "Miz Callie will be wondering what happened to us."

He put his hand on hers when she started to rise, stopping her from moving. She looked at him, and he took his hand away quickly.

"Just one thing—maybe you and Uncle Ned should talk to Miz Callie about this whole business. Get it all out in the open."

"Instead of sneaking behind her back to look at the will?" Apparently she had enough energy for one last spurt of anger.

His face tightened. "Give me a little credit, Cathy. I might not like it, but whatever you did, Jamie shouldn't suffer for it. I suspect Miz Callie would say the same. Talk to her." He stood, face taut, looking about ten feet tall. "I'll get Jamie."

He stalked off, leaving her feeling small and miserable.

True to her promise, Georgia had brought Lindsay over to play with Jamie when Lindsay got out of school that afternoon. At the moment, the two of them were engaged in creating what Lindsay said was going to be the best sand castle ever. Jamie dug away industriously, while Lindsay ran back and forth with buckets of water.

"Such energy." Georgia, sitting in the beach chair next to Cathy's, tilted her sun hat forward. "I don't know where they get it all."

Cathy managed to smile. To nod. When all she really wanted to do was hide someplace until she'd straightened out her tumbling thoughts and feelings. Dr. McMillan and Adam competed in her mind, their voices echoing.

…don't see any reason why we won't have excellent results…

…whatever you did, Jamie shouldn't suffer for it…

She'd like to shut out the voices long enough to think it through, but she couldn't.

"…and all the baby turtles came out of the nest in the sand and ran toward the ocean, like this." Lindsay, flat on her belly in the sand, gave an imitation of turtle flippers. "I bet there were a million of them."

Jamie sat back on his heels, looking skeptical. "A whole million?"

"Maybe not quite that many," Georgia interceded. "But it really was exciting. We walked alongside them until they got into the ocean, so nothing could bother them."

"Let's go." Lindsay jumped to her feet, looking ready to fly down the beach. "I'll show you where the nest was."

Cathy's heart clenched. Before she could speak, Georgia did.

"Not today," Georgia said. "You've got to get that sand castle finished before the tide turns."

"Oh, right." Lindsay squatted next to Jamie and began piling up sand.

"Sorry," Georgia said softly, under the cover of the murmuring tide and the children's voices. "She just didn't think about how hard it would be for Jamie to walk that far."

"Don't apologize. It's wonderful for Jamie to have her to play with. She's so open and bubbly he can't resist her."

"She is, isn't she?" Love filled Georgia's face when she looked at the little girl. "If you'd seen her when they first moved here, you wouldn't believe it was the same child. She was so tied up in grief for her mother that she could barely relate to anyone else."

"You've done a wonderful job with her, then."

"Not me," Georgia said. "Miz Callie helped her most of all. And Matt, once he realized the harm his own grief was doing to her."

"I didn't know." She hadn't even thought about it, and the realization shamed her. She'd been so obsessed with her own problems that she hadn't thought about anyone else's.

"Next year you and me will help Miz Callie with the turtle nests." Lindsay's high voice carried over the sand. "We'll do it together, okay?"

Cathy opened her mouth to speak, but it would be awkward to correct the child's assumption that they'd be here next year.

"Do you want me to say something to her?" Georgia seemed to interpret Cathy's thoughts correctly.

"No, that's all right. I'll remind Jamie later that we're just on a visit."

"It would be nice if it weren't just a visit," Georgia said. "Would you consider relocating here so you'd be near family? Surely that would be a help to you."

Georgia didn't have the faintest idea how difficult that would be for them. Certainly Grandpa could never get enough for the farm to even put a down payment on a house in this area. It was another example of how these people couldn't imagine what it was like to struggle just to get by.

"I don't think so. My grandfather's pretty set in his ways."

Georgia turned to look up at the house, and Cathy followed the direction of her gaze. Grandpa and Miz Callie sat side by side, heads together, talking. Even from this distance, she could read the relaxation in his figure.

"Looks as if he's pretty happy here at the moment," Georgia said. "And Miz Callie, too. She's been so determined to right that old wrong that it was really wearing on her. I guess maybe when we get older, we'll want to mend any mistakes we've made."

"Maybe so." She considered that. "I already regret a few bad ones."

"Me, too, as far as that goes," Georgia said. "Believe me, if I could go back and undo my first engagement, I would."

"I didn't know you'd been engaged before." Here was a new light on Georgia, who seemed to have it all together.

"Oh, yes. And he was a jerk, which doesn't say much for my judgment, does it?"

"Now you're with Matt, and he's definitely one of the good ones, from what I've seen of him."

"He surely is." Georgia's voice softened with love. "He's a man of integrity, like my daddy. Like Adam. I didn't realize how important that integrity was until I got involved with someone who didn't have any."

Cathy hoped she didn't betray anything at that mention of Adam. "Maybe that broken engagement wasn't a total loss, then, if it taught you that."

Georgia grinned. "You sound like Miz Callie. She always says the past is for learning from, not regretting."

"That's probably good advice, but not so easy to do. How do you stop regretting when you've made a big mistake?"

"I'm sorry." Georgia touched her arm lightly. "I didn't mean to remind you of your marriage."

Cathy shrugged. "It's not easy to forget. I

alienated my grandparents for the sake of a man who couldn't handle it when I produced a less-than-perfect child."

"He was a jerk," Georgia said warmly. "Just look at that beautiful child. Who wouldn't love him? You should hear Adam rave about how smart he is. I declare, it makes me jealous."

"He doesn't, does he?" She couldn't help being pleased at praise for her son, but it made her uncomfortable to think of Adam talking about Jamie that way.

"He surely does. He's grown so fond of that boy. Well, we all have, but especially Adam. Just as we've grown fond of you."

Strands, tightening around her. More people she could disappoint the way she'd disappointed everyone else. Her grandmother. Her grandfather. Paul.

Not Jamie, she thought, and the thought turned to prayer. *Please, Father, don't let me disappoint Jamie.*

Adam had come to the beach house that evening, despite telling himself that he should stay away. Even when he was on duty, outwardly busy, at the back of his mind he saw Jamie's face, screwed up not to cry when he was hurting. He felt the grip of Jamie's small hand on his.

He started up the stairs, determination in every

step. Jamie needed the surgery. Ned and Cathy couldn't pay for it. Ned was family. That meant the rest of them had to help, whether that was welcome or not.

This had nothing to do with the fact that Jamie reminded him of Juan, nothing to do with his complex feelings about Cathy. It wasn't affected by that arrest record in Cathy's past. All that mattered now was a hurting little boy who needed help.

Miz Callie came hurrying to greet him. "Adam, I didn't know you were stoppin' by tonight. This surely is a pleasure."

"Yes, ma'am, I just couldn't stay away." He kissed her cheek. "A little bird told me there was some pecan pie over here, unless y'all already ate it."

She patted his cheek. "Always some left for you, sugar."

"Adam! It's Adam!" Jamie appeared at the top of the stairs, wearing only his pajama bottoms.

Cathy pulled the pajama top over his head from behind. "Say hi to Adam. Then it's time for bed."

Jamie's bottom lip came out. "That's not fair. I want to see Adam. I want him to tuck me in."

"Jamie…" Cathy began.

"Okay by me." Adam went up the stairs two at the time. "I've just been thinking that's what I wanted, too." He scooped Jamie up in his arms, very aware of Cathy's eyes on him. "Which way, buddy?"

"That way." Jamie pointed. "The room that has the bunk beds in it, 'cept Mama won't let me sleep in the top bunk."

Adam carried him into what had always been the boys' bedroom and plopped him down on the bunk where the covers were turned back. "I used to sleep in this room when I came to stay with my grandmama, and the rule always was that you had to be seven to sleep in the top bunk. You seven yet?"

Jamie scrunched up his face. "Not yet. I'm only six."

"Well, you've got a ways to wait, then." He pulled the sheet up. The pajamas Jamie wore were faded to the point that he could barely make out the pattern of trains on them, and several inches too short. He'd have to do something about that.

As if she'd read his mind, Cathy reached out to smooth the pajama top down. "I declare, Jamie, you must be sprouting since you've been here. You're outgrowing your clothes."

He couldn't see Cathy's face, because it was turned toward the boy, but if he could, he knew he'd see embarrassment there. Cathy had been right to take him to task for not understanding what it was to try and make do the way she had to.

"Tell Adam good-night now, and then we'll have your story and prayers."

"I want Adam to read my story." Jamie flounced rebelliously on the bed. "Please, Adam."

"Sure thing," he said quickly, before Cathy could object. "Okay if I pick the book? I remember these. They were here when I was your age."

He picked through the children's books shoved into the bookcase between the sets of bunk beds. Two shelves held the chapter books that had occupied them on rainy days at the beach, but the third had a stack of picture books suitable for being read to.

He pulled out a battered copy of *The Little Engine that Could*. "This was one of my favorites when I was little."

Jamie, who looked as if he was about to protest that the story was for babies, closed his mouth and snuggled down on the pillow instead.

Adam flipped the book open, sitting on the bunk next to the boy. Cathy sank down on the rag rug next to the bed, her hand over Jamie's. From this angle he could see only the curve of her neck and the line of her jaw. It looked…vulnerable, somehow, just like Jamie's trusting eyes did. They both needed someone to take care of them.

He cleared his throat and began to read. The repetition of the simple story even made him feel drowsy. Small wonder that by the time the little engine reached its triumph, Jamie's eyes were at half-mast.

"Prayers now," Cathy said.

"Now I lay me down to sleep, I pray the Lord my soul to keep." Jamie finished the prayer, ending with God blesses for Mama and Grandpa, Miz Callie, Lindsay and Adam.

Adam discovered that there was a lump in his throat as he bent to kiss the boy's soft cheek. Jamie needed help, he thought again as he stood and followed Cathy out of the room. He was going to get it.

He and Cathy were alone for a brief moment at the top of the stairs. He might have said something about it then, but Cathy was already hurrying down. She obviously didn't want to have any private conversations with him. Hardly surprising.

The minute she saw them, Miz Callie bustled out to the kitchen, no doubt for the pecan pie.

Adam took the chair next to Uncle Ned. "How're you doing, sir? How is the knee?"

"Can't complain," Ned said. "That doctor's finally going to let me put some weight on it tomorrow."

"Don't rush things," Miz Callie said, coming back with plates of pie. Cathy followed her, carrying a tray laden with coffee pot and cups.

"She's babying me," Ned confided. "But seems like it makes her happy."

"Miz Callie always likes taking care of folks." Adam took a bite of the pie and felt the sweet, rich flavor fill his mouth. "Mmm, good pie."

"Sure is." Uncle Ned's glance flickered toward the big windows, beyond which dusk made the ocean a gray, moving mass. "You out on patrol today?"

Adam hid his surprise. It was the first time the man had shown any interest in what he did. "We did a loop down the Ashley and then down the coast this afternoon. Now much doing on a weekday except the commercial traffic."

Uncle Ned nodded. "Much smuggling going on? I remember when it was rumrunners."

"Not much of that anymore, but still plenty of smuggling. Drugs, sometimes weapons."

"Illegals? Not so much here as in Florida, I guess."

Ned couldn't know what a reminder that was. "I was stationed in Miami for a while. We saw a lot of it there. Here it's more rescue work."

"Guess so. Storm season now, even though it's been pretty quiet so far this year," Ned said. "Not pleasant, trying a rescue in high seas. Takes steady nerves."

Adam shrugged. "You know what we say in the service. 'You have to go out, but you don't have to come back.'"

Ned's hands tightened on the arms of the chair. "Right about that." His voice had turned gravelly.

Before he could pursue that, Cathy spoke.

"Grandpa. Miz Callie. There's something I'd like to tell you both."

Adam swung toward her, and the strain on her face stole his breath for a moment. He seemed to feel her in his arms again, her body shaking with sobs.

"What is it, girl?" Ned barked the words.

Cathy's fingers twisted together. She glanced at Miz Callie, then looked down at the floor. "Miz Callie, I…I thought I should tell you what I did." She took an audible breath. "I went in to the courthouse and looked up Grandpa's father's will. I'm sorry. I shouldn't have gone sneaking in there without telling anyone. I just thought…"

"Thought?" Ned's color darkened alarmingly. "Seems to me you didn't think at all. I don't know or care what that will said. I don't want anything from him. And you had no right—"

"Nonsense, Ned." Miz Callie interrupted him sharply. "Of course she had a right to know. She's family."

Cathy leaned toward her. "I shouldn't have done it behind your back. I'm sorry. I didn't know you very well yet then, and I hoped…"

"Well, of course you did." Miz Callie took Cathy's hands in hers and turned to Ned. "Stop sputtering, Ned. It's only natural that Cathy would want to know how the property was left, especially now, with Jamie needing an operation."

That reminder took the wind out of Ned's sails. He subsided, some of the ruddy color fading from his cheeks.

"By the time your daddy revised his will after your mama died, he thought you were dead." Miz Callie spoke directly to Ned. "Otherwise, he'd never have left everything to Richmond the way he did. I want you to understand that. Up 'til then, everything was divided between the two of you. I don't know what he might have said to you in a fit of anger, but he never thought about cutting you out."

"I don't want anything from him," Ned said again, but the words were softer, and those might have been tears lurking in his eyes.

"Well, want it or not, fair is fair," Miz Callie said briskly. "As soon as we found out that you were still alive, I told the lawyers to figure out what your share is. Soon as they can complete the paperwork, I'll be making it over to you."

Adam watched hope blossom in Cathy's face. There could be no doubt about what this meant to her.

"I told you I don't want it," Ned said, his color rising again. "I didn't come here for that."

That hope was gone again as quickly as it had come, leaving Cathy pale and drawn.

He had to do something. "Nobody thinks that," Adam said. "Maybe you don't want anything for yourself, but you're not going to turn it down for Jamie. He needs that surgery. You're not going to deny him that chance."

Ned stared at him, gaze belligerent for a moment. Then, finally, his gaze dropped. "Guess maybe you got a point there. The boy has to have his chance." He looked at Callie then. "I'm grateful."

Cathy made a small, maybe involuntary movement that brought his gaze to hers. She looked…she looked as if all her prayers had just been answered. Maybe they had.

Chapter Twelve

Cathy hung up the phone a few days later and stood staring blankly out at the morning sun slanting across the water.

"Cathy?" Miz Callie touched her arm. "What is it? Is something wrong?"

"Not wrong. Right. That was the doctor's office. They've had a cancellation, and they can do Jamie's surgery on Wednesday." She put her hand to her cheek. "I can't take it in."

Miz Callie put her arms around her. "Goodness gracious, that is wonderful news. Why, before you know it, that boy's going to be running around with the best of them."

"Thanks to you." A tear spilled over, and she wiped it away with her fingers.

"Not me," Miz Callie said. "Call it God's handiwork, putting the thought in my mind to find out what happened to Ned. And look at all that's come from it."

Cathy nodded, blotting away another tear. "Look at us, standing here and crying happy tears. We have company coming, remember?" Miz Callie had arranged to have a boyhood friend of Grandpa's come for a visit. He'd apparently helped her unravel the events of that last summer.

"Land, yes." Miz Callie glanced at the ship's clock on the wall. "Adam will be here with Benny any minute now. I can't tell you how excited Benny is—I thought he was going to jump through the phone at the idea of seeing his friend after all these years."

"I hope it won't be too much for Grandpa. That summer they were friends was an unhappy time for him in a lot of ways."

Miz Callie shook her head. "If there's one thing I've learned as I've gotten older, it's that the best way to look at the past is to sift through it for those bright moments. They'll come up, shining like a bit of beach glass in the sand, and you can just let the rest slip away."

Now Cathy was getting teary again. "I hope Grandpa can learn to see it that way."

"Give him time," Miz Callie said. "He's been hanging on to his grudges for a long while. He won't let them go easy, but I think this is a good step in that direction."

The sound of footsteps on the wooden stairs ended the conversation.

"You go get your grandpa now." Miz Callie shooed her toward the bedrooms. "I'll let them in."

Nodding, she hurried into the bedroom. Georgia had taken Jamie for the morning, so all she had to worry about right now was Grandpa. He was standing in front of the dresser, checking himself out in the mirror. "Do I look all right?" he demanded. "I don't want Benny to think I look like an old codger."

"You look handsome." She kissed his cheek. "Come on, now. I hear them coming in."

They walked into the living room together. Adam towered over Miz Callie and the elderly man he'd brought with him, and for a moment her heart seemed to skip a few beats. Grandpa stood very stiff, his arm as hard as a board under her hand.

And then the visitor was coming toward them, beaming, holding out his hand. "Ned! I tell you what, I never thought to see you again, you ole seadog. It's me, Benny. Don't you recognize me?"

Benny was small and spry, with a pair of snapping black eyes and cheeks like round, hard apples. He didn't just smile, he beamed with good humor and delight at seeing his old friend again.

Cathy felt the tension go out of her grandfather

as he reached out to pump Benny's hand. "How'm I supposed to recognize you? You got old. What happened to your hair?"

Benny ran a hand over his bald pate, grinning. "Hey, I still got my health. What's a little hair, I always say. And the ladies still like me fine."

"You're dreaming, that's what." Grandpa clasped him by the arm. "I never expected to see you again. Figured you were dead by now."

"Listen, if I could survive going along when you took that sailboat out in the storm, I can survive anything."

"You two sit down now." Miz Callie ushered them to chairs. "Ned, you need to get off that knee."

"You grew up bossy, Little Callie," he said, but he sat, leaning toward Benny, his face looking younger than it had in years. "You remember when we put out all those crab traps, Benny, and Cal Westing came along and messed with them?"

"I remember we got even with him but good." Benny smacked his lips. "Those were some of the best crabs I ever ate."

"Well, we don't have crab, but Miz Callie made some of her pecan tassies," Cathy said. "And how about some sweet tea?"

Benny nodded. "Sounds good to me."

She headed for the kitchen, to find Adam coming in behind her.

"I'll help you."

"It's all ready," she said, rushing the words. Being alone with Adam was dangerous to her peace of mind. "But I did want to tell you the good news. The doctor's office called this morning. They're going to do his surgery on Wednesday."

Adam whistled. "That is fast. Does Jamie know?"

"Not yet. Georgia's watching him this morning. I was afraid that this visit might upset Grandpa."

Adam picked up the tray holding the pitcher and glasses. "So far he seems happy. And Benny was just beside himself on the drive over. Good thing the drawbridge was down, or he might have tried to swim over."

"He's sweet, isn't he?" She took the platter of cookies Miz Callie had waiting. "I guess, at their age, there aren't that many people left who remember you as a kid."

He nodded, holding the swinging door open with his elbow so that she could go through. As she approached, she realized that the topic of conversation had changed. Miz Callie looked a little apprehensive as Benny leaned forward, gesturing with both hands.

"…and there we were, working our way up the boot of Italy. I was never so dirty and so tired in my life, not even when we used to go out shrimping all day. Sometimes I'd lean against a rock and imagine I was back on the boat with you, sun beating down on us, the waves rocking the boat beneath me. That'd give me enough strength to get up and walk another ten miles."

"So you went in the infantry. I always thought you'd join the Navy when you turned eighteen." Grandpa had never, so far as she knew, talked about the war, but he seemed to be easing in that direction now.

She glanced at Miz Callie and saw the apprehension she felt reflected there.

"Yeah, well, that's when we were gonna enlist together. After you left, well, my cousin was in the Army, so I figured that was a good enough reason."

"Maybe you were smart." Grandpa's face set in deeper lines. "Wasn't no picnic in the Navy, I can tell you."

"You on a destroyer?" Benny asked.

"PT boat in the Pacific." Grandpa's mouth clamped shut. When he looked that way, she knew better than to pursue a subject.

Benny, it seemed, wasn't intimidated. "I always figured maybe you guys in the Pacific had it easier, on those tropical islands with coconuts and hula dancers."

Grandpa snorted. "Never did see a hula dancer. And either the Japanese were shelling the islands or we were."

"You spend your whole war out there?"

Grandpa's hands tightened on the arms of his chair. "I don't want to talk about it."

Cathy exchanged glances with Adam, not liking the way Grandpa's voice had risen on the words.

"Suit yourself." Benny shrugged. "Me, I didn't like talking about it for a long time. Saw too many good men die. But the older I get, the better it feels when I get a chance to talk to someone who remembers. Not many of us left, y'know?"

"I know." Grandpa shook his head. "I knew a lot who didn't come back." He took a deep breath, and his face seemed to pale. "Fact is, my boat was sunk. I was the only survivor. Bobbed around in that ocean for days before they picked me up. Seemed like, by the time I got home again, I just wanted to get as far away from the ocean as I could get."

So she finally knew. That was what had brought him to the mountains.

"Yeah?" Benny seemed to find that hard to believe. "Me, all I wanted to do was get back to my regular life. Came right back to Charleston and stayed here. My wife, she wanted to go on one of them tours to Italy one time, and I told her to go if she wanted, but I'd seen enough of foreign parts to last me a lifetime. She settled on a trip to Myrtle Beach instead."

Grandpa's pallor seemed to be easing, and she

suspected that all Benny's chatter had been aimed at giving him time to get past the painful memory.

"If I'd tried that with my wife, she'd have boxed my ears." He shot a glance at Cathy. "Your grandma never took guff from anybody, did she?"

"No, sir, she didn't."

"Feisty, was she? I didn't think that was your type." Maybe Benny was remembering the woman Grandpa had loved and lost.

"If she hadn't been, we never would have got together," Grandpa said. "All I wanted was to be left alone. She was a widow with a young daughter, had a room to rent when I turned up, only half-human, way I remember it. She babied me and bullied me and brought me back to life again." He wiped away a tear. "I reckon God knew what he was doing when He led me to her door."

"Amen," Miz Callie said softly.

Cathy discovered that her cheeks were wet, and she hadn't even realized she was crying. She wiped her eyes, her gaze meeting Adam's. For a moment it seemed there was a line of empathy, of communion, between them.

And then he turned away, and it was gone.

Cathy heard a car crunch over the crushed shells of the driveway. "That'll be Adam, bringing Jamie back from Georgia's." She bent over her grandfather. He'd been sitting in the rocking chair since

Adam took Benny home, hardly speaking, and it was beginning to alarm her.

"Would you like to lie down in your room for a bit?"

"I'm fine where I am." He'd turned the chair to face the window, and once in a while he took a brooding glance in that direction. "Don't fuss."

She was trying not to. But that story he'd told, about those days drifting at sea, knowing all his shipmates were dead—well, it explained a lot that had puzzled her over the years about her grandfather. But telling it had taken an emotional toll on him.

She bit her lip. There had been so many changes in their lives in such a short period of time, and Grandpa had never been very good at dealing with change. If she'd made a mistake in urging him to come here—but what else could they have done? Once he had admitted who he was, the rest followed inevitably. She didn't doubt that if they hadn't come to Charleston, they'd have found Miz Callie on their doorstep.

She could hear Adam coming up the steps and went to open the door, forcing herself to smile. She'd assumed Georgia would be the one bringing Jamie back, but Adam and Georgia had made other plans. So Jamie was in Adam's company yet again, learning to depend upon him more every day.

It's dangerous to depend on someone that way.

The little voice at the back of her thoughts was persistent. Adam meant well where Jamie was concerned. She didn't doubt that. But sooner or later Adam would move out of his life, and Jamie would be devastated. Adam didn't understand what his casual friendship meant to a child like Jamie.

"Hey, Mama." Jamie started to chatter even before Adam put him down. "I had so much fun with Lindsay. We played games, and Cousin Georgia took us to the park, and we played in the sandbox, and then we went and saw some really big ships."

"Patriot's Point," Adam said in response to her questioning look. "Georgia took them by there to see the ships." He sent a cautious glance toward her grandfather, but he was staring out the window again.

Cathy spread her hands, shrugging. She had no idea what was going through her grandfather's mind right now, but whatever it was, it seemed all they could do was leave him alone.

But Jamie didn't know that. He made his way to the rocker as quickly as his braced legs would carry him. "I saw a really big ship, Grandpa."

Grandpa seemed to tear his gaze away from the window with an effort. He rested his hand on Jamie's head. "You did, did you? Did Lindsay go, too?"

"Yes, sir. And we stopped for ice cream afterward.

I had chocolate, and Lindsay had strawberry, and Cousin Georgia said she'd just have what was left over from ours."

"That's good." Grandpa looked at her. "Did you tell the boy yet about Wednesday?"

"Not yet." She'd really prefer to wait until after Adam was gone. She was too aware of his often-critical gaze on her to be comfortable. And the times when he forgot to be critical were even worse, because then the feelings she didn't want to have broke free of her control.

"Well, tell him," Grandpa said, impatient as always.

"What about?" Jamie caught on instantly, of course. "What are we going to do on Wednesday, Mama?"

She crossed the room to sit in Miz Callie's usual chair, drawing Jamie close to her. His eyes were wide in expectation of some treat.

"The doctor's office called, and on Wednesday, the doctor is going to be able to do your operation. Isn't that good? You'll be—"

Jamie's face clouded. "But I don't want to. Mama, do I have to?"

"I know it's a little bit scary, sugar, but you're going to be fine. I'll be right there with you."

"But I don't want to. I want to play with Lindsay, and Adam promised he'd take me out on his boat, and now I have to miss everything on account of my stupid legs." He burst into tears.

"Sugar, it's all right." She drew him onto her lap, trying to hold him close, but he pushed away, denying the comfort she wanted to give. And she tried to deny the hurt that caused her.

"I know you don't want to miss things." She'd expected tears over the thought of being in the hospital, not over that. "But all those things will still be there when you get out of the hospital."

Jamie shook his head, tears spilling faster.

"Hey, listen, Jamie." Adam knelt next to them, putting his hand on Jamie's back. "I know this is tough news. But you know, sometimes you have to give up something you want right now for the sake of something better later."

Jamie didn't seem comforted by that thought, but he was listening, at least. "Like what?" He sniffled a bit and wiped his tears on his sleeve.

"Well, like one time I really wanted to get a new bicycle, and I was saving up for it. So when my friends wanted to go to the movies or spend money on video games, I'd think about that new bike, and I'd save my money instead. I knew I'd rather have that bike later than play some game now." He stroked Jamie's back gently as he spoke. "That's like you. You know you'd rather have your legs be all better because of the operation, even if you have to give up some fun now. Right?"

"I...I guess." Jamie didn't sound all that sure of it.

"Besides, you don't have to give up the boat ride. I'm off duty tomorrow, so we can take a picnic lunch and go for a ride after church, if it's okay with your mama."

"Can we, Mama?" The sunshine broke through the rain clouds.

She was apprehensive on so many levels she didn't know where to begin. She didn't want Jamie spending so much time with Adam, learning to love and rely on him. She didn't want the enforced intimacy that this trip implied. And she wasn't sure what Grandpa would think about it.

Adam was already turning to her grandfather. "Would you like to go along, sir? I'd love to show you my boat."

"Not this time." His response was negative, but it wasn't as sharp as Cathy expected. "Maybe... maybe I'll go sometime."

"I can go, can't I, Grandpa?" Jamie, having failed to get an answer from her, appealed to a higher authority.

"I reckon so." There was a shadow of apprehension in his eyes, but he smiled. "I guess you can't be safer than with the Coast Guard."

Something tightened in Adam's face at that, gone again so quickly that Cathy thought she'd imagined it.

"Okay with you, Cathy?" Adam was still kneeling next to her, his face very close to hers.

"Please, Mama." Jamie put his hands on her cheeks, as if he'd force a nod from her. "Say yes."

"Yes," she said, dropping a kiss on his nose. "Yes, we'll go. Say thank you to Cousin Adam for thinking of it."

Jamie gave her a throttling hug and then threw himself at Adam. "Thank you, thank you, thank you."

She couldn't say no, not when Adam had asked right in front of Jamie. Whether it was safe or not, she was going to be spending the afternoon with Adam.

Jamie was sound asleep on the bench seat of the boat. Adam flexed his fingers on the wheel and slowed as they approached the No Wake zone. With Cathy sitting opposite the boy, she was only a couple of feet way. They were alone, in effect, and he wasn't so sure that was a good idea.

The breeze off the water caught Cathy's hair, blowing it away from her face, and she closed her eyes, tilting her chin up as if enjoying the sensation. She had a strong face, not conventionally pretty but with the kind of bone structure that would still be attractive when she was Miz Callie's age.

That strength had fooled him at first. He'd

mistaken it for hardness. But he'd soon seen the vulnerability beneath it.

This was a woman he could love. He looked at the idea carefully, not sure he wanted to believe it. Every time he thought he had her figured out, something new came up. How could he be sure there wasn't another surprise around the corner?

And there was the matter, still unexplained, of that arrest record back in Atlanta. If he asked her, point-blank, what would she say? Maybe there was some reasonable explanation.

But he couldn't. He'd agreed with Hugh that he would wait until Hugh found out a bit more. But the days were ticking past. Cathy and Jamie were assuming a bigger part in his life, and still Hugh hadn't learned anything else.

Besides, even if that arrest were explained, what did he think would happen? Maybe most people, deceived by his exterior, thought him a rock, but the rock was beginning to crack. He was haunted by his indecisiveness the day they'd caught the smugglers. How could he ask anybody else to trust him when he didn't trust himself?

He glanced at Jamie. The boy slept heavily, intensely almost, as if not bothered by either the bulky lifejacket or the metal braces.

"He had a good day," Cathy said. "Thank you for giving it to him."

"It was a pleasure. My pleasure, as a matter of

fact. I loved seeing the island through his eyes."
He'd taken them to Miz Callie's island, where she
planned her nature preserve. The picnic pavilion
had already been built, and signs explained various
aspects of the island's natural life.

"It's amazing, what Miz Callie has done there.
I know Jamie will never forget this visit."

*Will you, Cathy? Did you know I wanted to stop
and kiss you a dozen times?*

"The project has really shaped up since Miz
Callie made the decision early this summer," he
said. "I understand the memorial stone is nearly
finished. All that remains is to decide on the lettering. Are Miz Callie and your grandfather still
arguing about that?"

Cathy's lips curved. "They are. It's kind of cute
to listen to them. He insists it can't be a memorial, 'cause he's not dead yet, and he doesn't want
anything named after him anyway, 'cause all he
managed to do was survive."

"And Miz Callie's determined that he deserves
it, wanting to show everyone the truth about him,"
he added, familiar with that side of the argument.
"Who do you think is going to win?"

"Since they're about equally stubborn, I don't
have a clue. Did you know that your cousin
Amanda wants to write an article about him for
the newspaper?"

He nodded, the tension he'd been feeling easing

away. Talking about someone else was far better than risking talking about themselves. "I hope he'll let her do it. She's been in on this practically from the beginning, and she really wants to tell Ned's story."

Cathy's face sobered. "I doubt he'll want her to write about the story he told us yesterday. I can't begin to imagine what that was like." She glanced at the water, and a shiver seemed to move over her.

"He had a rough time of it. The torture of losing his crew would be far worse than anything physical."

She nodded, brushing a strand of hair back behind her ear. The wind promptly teased it out again. "It was hard for him to tell us, but it explained a lot that I never understood about him."

"He must be doing better. He didn't raise any objection to my bringing the two of you out on the boat."

"He has confidence in the Coast Guard as represented by you."

"What do you mean by that?" His doubts about himself made the question sharp, and he instantly regretted giving that much away.

Cathy blinked, and her lips tightened at his tone. "Just that he sees what everyone does in you. That you're the rock of the family."

"That's nothing but a rumor, started by my sister."

He tried to turn it away lightly. The marina was in sight, and he slowed. Soon enough, this awkward conversation would be over.

"I know that's not true." She looked at him, seeming to measure his character. "Most people would say that was admirable, always being the perfect one."

Something about that tone nettled him. "I take it you're not one of them."

She shrugged. "It makes other people feel as if they can never live up to your standards."

"I don't set myself up as a gold standard for anyone." His normally slow temper was beginning to get the better of him. "At least I've never been—"

He stopped, appalled at himself. He'd been ready to blurt out something about that police record.

"What?" She swung around, facing him fully, every line in her body straight and stiff. "What are you implying about me?"

"Nothing. I wasn't implying anything."

"At least you've never been what?"

"Nothing." He could tell she wasn't buying it. He never had been able to lie convincingly.

"You think you know something discreditable about me. The least you can do is face me honestly with it and give me a chance to explain."

He couldn't keep on denying it. That wasn't fair

to either of them. "All right. At least I've never been arrested."

She stared at him for a moment, eyes darkening, her face very pale. "You know about what happened in Atlanta."

"I know you were arrested for robbing a pharmacy."

"You investigated me. I should have expected that, shouldn't I?" She wielded her anger against him, but it didn't hide the pain in the depths of her eyes.

His jaw hardened. "I have to protect Miz Callie." He wasn't going to apologize for that.

"Miz Callie doesn't need protecting from me." She threw the words at him. "You want to know what happened? I'll tell you. I robbed that store because my son had to have medicine. Because that clerk stood there and told me I'd have to do without the croup medicine he needed to help him breathe because I was two dollars short of having enough to pay for it." Her voice broke with remembered grief. "There it was, a row of those white boxes on the shelf behind the counter, and she wouldn't let me have it because I was two dollars short."

"Cathy, you don't have to—"

"No. You wanted to hear, so you'll hear." Her fingers pressed against the edge of the control console, white with strain. "All I could think about was Jamie, struggling to breathe. She turned her back on me and went to wait on someone more worthy. And I reached across that counter and grabbed it and ran." She put her hand up, rubbing her forehead. "I'm not proud of it. I know it was wrong, and I've confessed it. But if I were in that situation again, I can't say that I wouldn't do the same."

He put his hand out, grasping hers in mute sympathy, letting the boat bob at the mercy of the current. "What happened to you?"

"I was caught, of course." She tried to smile, but it was a pitiful effort. "I wasn't a very good thief. I was arrested. They let my neighbor take care of Jamie, but if Grandpa hadn't come, hadn't gotten a lawyer for me, hadn't told the judge he'd be responsible for us—well, I don't know what would have happened. I'd have ended up in jail, maybe, and Jamie in foster care. I owe him so much." She took a ragged breath. "But when I think about the way he looked at me—well, maybe jail would have been better."

His fingers tightened on hers. "Don't say that. He loves you. He understands."

She shook her head, her face filled with sorrow. "He doesn't. He's never forgiven me. Things have never really been right for us since then."

He'd seen for himself the way Uncle Ned treated her sometimes, so he couldn't go on denying it. "I'm sorry, Cathy."

"Right." She straightened, rubbing the back of

her neck as if it hurt. "You're sorry. I'm sorry. At least now you know my terrible secret. You won't have to investigate me anymore."

The bitterness in her voice cut him to the heart. And yet what could he say? He'd done what he had to do.

But it had placed a wall between them, and he suspected it was one he could never get over.

Chapter Thirteen

"Mama, where's Adam? Isn't he coming today?"

Cathy turned from the gray, rain-swept view, looking at her son with slight exasperation. Just what she'd feared would happen was occurring. Jamie was growing dependent on Adam, and he was rapidly getting past the stage at which she could kiss every hurt and make it better.

"I'm sure he's on duty today, Jamie." She'd said the same thing in various ways at least a dozen times already.

"He'll be out in his patrol boat, looking for folks in trouble on a day like this," Grandpa said, laying aside his newspaper.

"I wish he was here," Jamie said, his voice as close to a whine as he ever got.

Grandpa exchanged glances with Cathy. They both knew, only too well, that it was the prospect of going into the hospital on Wednesday that had brought this on. If it hadn't been raining, she could have distracted him with a trip to the beach.

"Tell you what," Grandpa said. "Go find one of those games you and Lindsay were playing. You can teach me how to play."

That brightened Jamie's face. He hurried to the shelf where Miz Callie had stacked boxes of children's games. "You'll like Chutes and Ladders, Grandpa. I'll show you how to play. Maybe when Lindsay comes, all three of us can play."

She had no idea whether Lindsay would show up after school on such a wet day, but they'd deal with that problem when it was necessary. She helped Jamie pull a small table and chair into place, making sure the table legs were nowhere near Grandpa's still-swollen knee.

"There now, you're all set." She glanced at the clock. "I'll just do a few things in the kitchen before Miz Callie gets back."

Miz Callie let her do little enough around the house. At least she could unload the dishwasher before she got back from her meeting at church. With a little luck, Jamie would be so preoccupied with the game that he'd forget to ask where Adam was for a while, at least.

She stacked plates on the countertop and wiped off silverware, but the routine chores didn't serve to soothe her nerves or erase the memories that clung like cobwebs to her mind.

Talking to Adam yesterday about that awful time had brought it all back, and for a moment she felt a fierce resentment toward him, for making her think about it.

And not just think. She'd dreamt about it last night. Funny how in a dream all the emotions were as sharp and real as if they were happening right at the moment. She'd relived the terror, the complete and utter helplessness of being locked up, the panic of not knowing if Jamie was all right. Her life had spun totally out of her control. If Grandpa hadn't come...

But he had come, and thanks to him, she and Jamie were safe and together. But that safety had come at a cost. Grandpa had never looked at her the same way again.

She braced her hands against the counter. She'd emptied the dishwasher and put everything away without even realizing she was doing it, thanks to her preoccupation with the past.

The ring of the doorbell took her by surprise. "It's Lindsay," Jamie squealed. "I told you she'd come."

She walked quickly back to the living room. "It might be someone else."

The door opened before she could reach it, and Georgia and Lindsay spilled in out of the rain.

"Goodness, it's wet out." Georgia grabbed Lindsay before she could bolt toward Jamie. "Wipe your feet first, darlin', and hang up your raincoat."

"I will." Lindsay slid out of her raincoat, and Georgia caught it before it could hit the floor. In an instant Lindsay had wiped her shoes on the braided rug inside the door and hurried across to Jamie and Grandpa.

"Oh, boy, Chutes and Ladders. Can I play, too?"

"You can take my place," Grandpa offered.

"It's more fun with three," Lindsay said, tilting her head to the side. "Please play with us."

Grandpa smiled, no more immune to Lindsay's pleading than he was to Jamie's.

"Thanks so much for bringing her over." She helped Georgia hang up wet coats. "I thought maybe you wouldn't want to come out on such a wet day."

"Better to come so the two of them can complain about the rain together," Georgia said. "Any chance of a glass of tea? I've been running errands, and I'm parched."

"I'm sure there's a fresh pitcher. You know your grandmother—tea in the fridge and cookies in the cookie jar."

"When I grow up, I want to be just like her." Georgia grinned, following Cathy to the kitchen.

"I'll get some milk for the children as well." Cathy lifted the carton from the refrigerator.

"Good idea. We came straight from school, so Lindsay hasn't had a snack." Georgia took the lid off the bear-shaped cookie jar and began to fill a plate. "Lucky the rain wasn't yesterday. Did you have a good time with Adam?"

It took an effort to block out the ending that had spoiled the day. "Very nice. Jamie loved going on the boat."

"Funny," Georgia said. "I asked Adam, and he very nearly bit my head off."

Cathy felt her color rising. "I don't know why—"

Georgia clasped her hand warmly. "I hope we're friends as well as cousins, Cathy. I won't pry, but if you want to talk about anything, I'd like to listen. Something certainly has my brother in a tailspin. Not that that's not good for him. He's usually all too sure of himself."

Adam the rock, she thought but didn't say. "We... quarreled, I guess." A little flame of anger came up as she remembered why. "Adam had been investigating my past."

"I'm sorry." Georgia's brown eyes were warm with sympathy. "I guess I'm not really surprised, though. Adam feels responsible, because he's the one who found Uncle Ned. I'm sure he was just trying to protect Miz Callie, even though anybody could see she doesn't need protecting from you. Please don't be mad at him."

She managed a smile. "I'll try."

They carried the milk and cookies into the other room, and Lindsay's eyes brightened at the sight. "I love Miz Callie's pecan tassies. They're my favorite cookies in the whole world." She passed the plate politely to Grandpa and Jamie before taking one herself. "Did you know that my daddy and Georgia are getting married?"

Grandpa nodded gravely. "Seems to me I heard that."

"Then we'll all be related," Lindsay said. "I never had aunts and uncles and cousins before, but now I will. And Miz Callie will be my real grandmother." She took a bite of cookie and spoke around it. "Someone at school said she wouldn't be, but I asked Miz Callie, and she said she would."

"Miz Callie is always right," Grandpa said. "It's just like Cathy. Somebody might say she's my stepgranddaughter, but she's really my real granddaughter."

Her heart swelled at the unexpected words, and tears clouded her vision for a moment. "Thank you, Grandpa," she said, her voice choked.

He held out a hand to her, and she took it. "Been doing a lot of thinking since I've been here—about what I did with my life since I left. It made me realize something. Seems to me I did to you exactly the same thing my father did to me…trying to make you do what I wanted instead of listening to you."

She shook her head, her throat tight. "But you were right."

"Being right is small comfort when it comes between you and the ones you love." He focused on her, and it was as if they were alone in the room. "I'm sorry I let you down, Cathy. I hope you'll forgive me."

She put her arms around him, the burden she'd been carrying so long slipping away. "I already have, Grandpa."

"Everything is set up for tomorrow, so you're not to worry." Delia, Adam's mother, gave a wry smile at her own words as she drove Cathy and Jamie back to the beach house. "Well, that's silly, I know. You'll worry." She glanced in the rearview mirror at Jamie in the backseat. "But not about the arrangements, at least."

"I can't thank you enough. You've thought of everything, it seems."

Delia had taken them for all the pretests today, tackling the maze of labs and offices with the ease of familiarity. More than that, she'd choreographed everything for the next few days, making sure transportation was easily available, that someone would be with Grandpa when she couldn't be, that someone else was always on call in case anything was needed.

"To tell you the truth, I love to organize things," Delia said. "And people. My children always accused me of trying to organize them."

Cathy tried to focus on Delia's voice instead of on thoughts of the surgery coming at them too fast. "A mother can't help doing that."

"Hmm." Delia frowned at an out-of-state car which seemed to have gotten itself into the wrong lane, blocking her turn-off for a moment. "I suppose maybe I did take it to extremes. I'd have welcomed a little bit of naughtiness in Adam, and considerably more responsibility in Cole. Still, I suppose they were just living out the personalities they were born with."

Cathy pondered that. Had Adam really been born with that predisposition, or was it the result of being the oldest son in a military family? She didn't doubt that he'd had ideals of duty and sacrifice drummed into him from the cradle. While she admired the man who'd resulted from that, all that perfection was a bit hard for an ordinary flawed person to live up to.

"They're all different from the day they're born," Delia said. "You'll see that when you have another child."

That startled her into an admission she seldom

made, even to herself. "I don't think that will happen."

"Really?" Delia's voice lilted in surprise. "You're such a good mother I figured you wanted a houseful."

She glanced in the rearview mirror to be sure Jamie was still completely wrapped up in the small electronic game Delia had brought him. "The doctors can't really say what causes Jamie's condition. Even if I married again, I don't know that a man would be willing to take that chance."

Delia pulled up at the house. She turned toward Cathy, her expression serious. "The right man would. And there's always genetic counseling, to help you make a decision about whether or not to have other children."

She hadn't expected such sage, sympathetic advice from Delia. Obviously there was much more to Adam's mother than her polished, elegant exterior suggested.

"Maybe you're right." She didn't think so, but it was the polite thing to say. She started to open the door.

Delia stopped her with a hand on her arm. "I won't keep you, but—just don't give up too easily if there's something you've set your heart on."

Before she could react to that surprising bit of advice, Delia was turning around to say goodbye to Jamie.

"Thank you for my present, Cousin Delia." He held the game close as Cathy helped him out of the car.

"You're welcome, sugar." Delia wiggled her fingers at him. She glanced behind her as another car turned the corner. "There comes my son, I see. Cathy, you tell him not to go messing around with my schedule, y'heah?"

Cathy's heart seemed to have taken on a new routine of its own. "I'll tell him. And Delia—thank you so much. For everything."

She stepped back from the car. Delia pulled away, giving a little beep on the horn that was probably meant as a greeting for her son, who pulled into the space she'd vacated.

She could hardly walk into the house and ignore him, but her breath was doing strange things, and she had a cowardly wish to run away. She hadn't seen Adam since she'd been forced into telling him her deepest shame. How was she going to look at him without seeing that reflected in his eyes?

"Adam, you came," Jamie exclaimed, holding up his arms to Adam as if it were the most natural thing in the world. "Look what your mama gave me."

Adam lifted him, examining the handheld game with apparent interest. "That's really cool. I might have known my mama would get in there with the perfect gift. All I could think of to bring you was some new pajamas." He handed a bag to Cathy.

"You didn't need—" she began.

"I wanted to," he said firmly. "Besides, any guy who's going to spend a couple of days in the hospital needs some new pajamas so he looks cool."

"What are they, Mama?" Jamie wiggled, reaching.

Cathy opened the bag, pulling out three pairs of pajamas, each pair with a different cartoon character. "Wow, look at these, Jamie. You really will be cool in these."

Jamie grabbed the top pair, clutching it and the game against his chest. "I love you, Cousin Adam."

Adam put his arms around her son in a huge hug. "I love you, too, little guy." His eyes met Cathy's, and her heart seemed to stop.

Adam could feel the tension under Cathy's smiles and light chatter. He hung around, despite suspecting that she'd prefer his absence to his company. He wasn't sure he was helping any, but at least he was trying. He owed that to the child who'd said he loved him.

Memories of that other hurting child tried to intrude, and he shut them out. This was about Jamie.

Jamie was finally in bed and asleep in a pair of

his new pajamas. Adam watched Cathy walk across to the sliding glass doors and stand staring out.

Miz Callie sat in quiet conversation with Cathy's grandfather. She caught his glance and nodded toward Cathy.

Miz Callie didn't know what had happened between them on Sunday. She didn't realize that he was probably the last person capable of comforting Cathy just now.

Still, he had to try. Murmuring a silent prayer for guidance, he went to stand beside her.

She didn't turn, didn't acknowledge that he was there. Just stared out at beach and ocean. The sun had set, but a golden glow still lingered, as if reluctant to leave.

Cathy turned slightly, and he realized that the bright demeanor she'd maintained for Jamie had cracked right across. His heart ached for the worry in her eyes.

He touched her arm lightly. "Let's go outside for a bit."

He expected an argument. He didn't get it. Maybe she was too swamped with worry to do anything but agree. In any event, she nodded, and pushed the door open.

It was one of those clear, cool evenings that reminded you that eventually, even here in the low-country, winter would come. Cathy didn't seem to notice. She went down the stairs to the beach and turned right—maybe simply because that was easiest.

They walked without speaking for probably ten minutes, until the silence began to wear on him. He wanted—needed, really—to let her know he was sorry for pushing her to tell him more than she'd been ready to. But was it fair to burden her with anything else when she was carrying so much already?

Miz Callie would say there was never a bad time to say you were sorry.

He stopped, his hand on her arm halting her, too. "I'm sorry. About Sunday. I shouldn't have made you talk about it. I made things harder for you, and I'm sorry."

She looked at him then, misery darkening her eyes. "It doesn't matter now. I can't change the past. And I know your loyalty is to your family."

"You and Jamie are family now."

She shook her head. "Not really. Whatever you say, no matter how kind you all are, we're not a part of you the way my grandfather is."

"Of course you are."

"No. He shares a past with you. We don't. And I don't want Jamie to depend on you too much. I don't want him hurt."

"I would never hurt Jamie. How can you think that?"

"Don't you see?" Her face seemed to come

alive with passion. "Don't you understand? Jamie loves you. I don't want him to lose anyone else he loves."

"Cathy—"

"He was only two and a half the last time he saw his father. I thought—I hoped—maybe he was young enough that it wouldn't hurt him too much, but I was wrong. He was bereft."

He could read what lay behind that. Guilt. Cathy felt she was to blame for Jamie losing his father.

"Let's be clear about something. I'm not like Jamie's father. I don't walk away when the going gets rough, and I resent being compared to him."

She stared at him, maybe shaken by his vehemence.

"Maybe it's not just Jamie you're worried about. Maybe it's yourself."

"No. That's not so."

She looked so distraught that he felt like a jerk for having said it. He shouldn't be talking like that to her when she was already upset.

"Forget that." He tried to smile. "I shouldn't have said it. I didn't mean anything except that you can count on us. We won't let you down."

That was an unfortunate choice of words. He seemed to see the boy in the water again, the blood that surrounded him. How could he promise he wouldn't let her down when he didn't know if he could count on himself?

This wasn't the time to think about himself, only about Cathy and Jamie.

He bent to kiss her cheek lightly. "Jamie's going to be all right. I know. I promise."

Chapter Fourteen

Cathy glanced at her watch, checking it against the wall clock in the pediatric surgery waiting room. How many other mothers had sat here, watching the minutes tick away, hoping and praying?

Grandpa covered her hand with his. "It hasn't been that long, sugar. Don't you start fretting already."

"Jamie was so brave when they wheeled him away," Miz Callie said, as if to remind her that she must be brave, too. "He's such a fine boy. We're all so proud of him."

"He's going to be all right," Delia said. "I know it. Just think about all the people who are praying for him."

"All the family." Miz Callie clasped Cathy's other hand. "All those folks from church. Probably some others that we don't even know about, taking a minute today to say a prayer for that precious little boy."

"I know," she whispered. The lump in her throat was the size of a boulder when she thought of all those prayers rising to Heaven for her son.

Delia gave Adam an irritated glance. He'd been here since dawn, and he'd spent most of the time standing at the window, staring out over black-tar roofs. Was he messing up Delia's schedule, Cathy wondered? She didn't doubt that Delia had planned everyone's movements for today.

"Georgia will be along in about an hour," Delia said, like an echo of her thoughts. "And Ashton will come later, too. He suddenly decided that Jamie must have a replica of a Coast Guard cutter, and he went clear over to West Ashley to get it." Her tone was that of a woman baffled by the actions of her menfolk.

"That's so nice of him," Cathy said, trying to concentrate on anything but the slow movement of the clock.

"Well, it is, but it's also true that he hates hospitals. When Adam had his tonsils out, he did exactly the same thing, remember, Adam? He finally admitted that he'd rather drive to Timbuktu than sit waiting."

Adam nodded. "I guess. Mostly I remember the ice cream. And the bread pudding Miz Callie made for me."

Delia got up. "I declare, you're about as useful in a hospital as your daddy was, standing there propping that windowsill up. You come along with me and we'll get some coffee for everyone. You can help me carry it." Linking her arm with his, she didn't give him a chance to argue but tugged him out of the room.

"She knows being here upsets him," Miz Callie said, when the door had swung shut behind them. "She's just trying to keep him busy."

"I know." But was that all? Adam seemed more upset than she would have expected. He seemed so confident that the surgery would be successful that she didn't think he was having doubts about that. It was something else, something deeper, that troubled him.

And she couldn't imagine why she was even thinking about Adam when all her heart was bound up in what was happening to Jamie in that operating room. Apparently there was room for both of them.

The door opened, and Georgia peeked inside. Seeming reassured when she didn't see her mother, she came in, taking the seat Delia had vacated. "Don't tell Mama I came before I was supposed to," she said. "I couldn't wait any longer. Have you heard anything yet?"

"Nothing yet." The words sounded hollow to her,

and she tried to rally. "But the surgeon said it would be two to three hours at least."

Georgia nodded. "If they started on time, it shouldn't be too awfully long. Where's Adam?"

"He went with your mama to get some coffee for us," Miz Callie said. "So she's going to know you're off the schedule."

"Bother the schedule." Georgia blew out an exasperated breath. "The reason I went to USC in Columbia instead of the College of Charleston was so I could get off the schedule."

Miz Callie reached across Cathy's lap to pat Georgia's hand. "Your mama means well. You know that the more she cares, the more she can't resist the urge to organize."

Georgia grinned. "That must mean she really likes you, Cathy. The schedule for the next couple of days was so complicated she put it on a spreadsheet."

They were talking nonsense to keep her from worrying, she knew that. But all the same, it was comforting.

Miz Callie clucked her tongue. "I guess we shouldn't be rattling on like this now. We're bothering Cathy."

"No, you're not bothering me at all. You're making me feel like I'm part of the family, even though I'm not blood kin to you."

"You are part of the family," Miz Callie said

firmly. "Family isn't about blood. It's about feelings. We love you and Jamie, and that makes you kin."

Grandpa cleared his throat, and she thought there were tears in his eyes. "That's right."

The door swung open again, and Cathy's nerves snapped to attention. But it was Delia and Adam, carrying coffee. Delia stiffened at the sight of Georgia.

"You're not supposed to be here yet. I didn't want Cathy to start feeling overwhelmed by Bodines."

"I dropped Lindsay at school, and then I just had to come." Georgia got up to give her seat to her mother. "Cathy doesn't mind, do you?"

She shook her head. "I'm glad to have you here."

"Well, now that we're all settled, let's have prayer together." Miz Callie's tone was brisk. "Sit down here, all of you, and hold hands."

Clearly the family did what Miz Callie instructed when she got that tone in her voice. Adam pulled chairs into a circle. Miz Callie's hand was frail and soft, but it held Cathy's firmly. And on the other side, Grandpa's work-worn hand clasped hers.

"Dear Father, we come to You in agreement, holding up our dear Jamie for Your blessing. We ask that You be with the doctors and nurses who attend him, guiding their hands and their thoughts. We beg that You give him strength and send Your healing through him, making him whole. We ask that You be with us and help us to be strong for him. In Jesus's name, Amen."

For a moment Cathy clung to their hands, not willing to let go. She felt an incredible lightness, as if the spirit of God had been moving through them.

The lightness faded slowly, but the comfort didn't go away. Miz Callie was right. God was there for her to lean on.

People moved around. Georgia scanned notices tacked on to a bulletin board. Adam resumed his position at the window, staring out. Finally Cathy couldn't stand it any longer. She got up and went to him.

"You were right," she said softly. "They really are family."

His smile chased some of the worry from his face. "I'm glad you see that."

There was more she wanted to say. More she wanted him to understand. But this wasn't the time—

"Cathy." Georgia's voice sounded an alarm.

She looked across the room. The surgeon stood here, his mask still hanging around his neck.

"Miz Norwood?" He focused on her and began to smile. "Good news. The surgery went well, very well indeed. I think we're looking at a complete success."

"Will he walk?" Grandpa's voice was strained.

"Walk? It's going to take a lot of therapy and hard work, but he's not only going to walk. He's going to be running around with the best of them."

"Thank You, Father," Miz Callie said, and Cathy could only echo the words, smiling through her tears.

Thank You, Father.

Adam sat in the chair farthest from Jamie's hospital bed. He ought to be closer. Ought to be comforting the boy during those times when he woke from his uneasy doze.

He couldn't seem to do that without seeing that other boy, seeing the blood, knowing he was responsible. He fought to shake away the feeling, but it clung to him.

"Should I switch the television off?" he murmured.

Cathy shook her head. "I think the background noise is helping him sleep." She smoothed the sheet over Jamie's small chest, avoiding the area of his hips, where the surgery had been.

She was so strong and so gentle. She'd looked lost when she was waiting for the results of the surgery, but once she was with her son again, she was a different person. All her strength had come soaring back.

The rest of the family had left over an hour ago.

They'd be in and out tomorrow, of course. Maybe Miz Callie would be able to persuade Cathy to go home and rest for an hour or so then.

Nobody had even tried that tonight. Cathy would sleep, if she did, on the narrow cot in Jamie's room. Adam doubted she'd close her eyes at all.

Cathy drooped a little, resting her cheek on her palm, and his heart twisted.

"Why don't you stretch out on the cot for a bit? I'll watch him."

She came alert instantly. "I'm fine. You can go on home, you know."

It was what he thought he wanted, but he couldn't do it.

Jamie stirred, maybe awakened by their voices, his eyes flickering. "Mama."

"It's all right. I'm here, darlin'." She stroked his face.

"It hurts." Jamie's voice wavered. "Mama, it hurts me."

The words stabbed him to the heart. He couldn't watch Jamie in pain and be unable to ease it.

"I'm ringing for the nurse, sugar." She suited the action to the words. "She's going to give you something to make the hurt go away."

"Not a shot." Jamie's eyes opened wide. "I hate to have a shot."

"No, no, she'll put it in the medicine that's

already going in your arm. You won't feel anything, I promise."

Adam stood, remembering when he'd told Cathy that he wasn't like her husband. But wasn't he doing the same thing? Running away? "I'm going to the snack bar for a coffee. Can I bring you something?"

"No, thanks." Cathy's eyes were shadowed. She probably knew exactly what he was doing and despised him for it.

He couldn't help it. He turned and pushed his way blindly out of the room.

He headed down the hallway, not sure where he was going. Then he spotted the metal placard on a door. *Chapel. Welcome.*

He pushed the door open and went inside. The room was very plain and dimly lit—just a few padded benches facing a simple wooden cross. No one else was there. He could be alone to regain his composure.

He slipped onto the nearest bench and then, impelled by something stronger than he was, slid down to his knees. Pain rolled through him, pummeling him like a tidal wave. He'd tried to deal with this on his own. Tried and failed, again and again.

He'd been following the rules. No one in the service would fault him for that.

But he faulted himself.

"I'm sorry." The words came out with difficulty. "I'm sorry. I followed the rules, but I didn't go the extra mile. I didn't follow my instincts, and people were hurt by that."

They were the words he hadn't been able to say for the past year. They seemed to burn through him, painful but cleansing.

"I'm sorry. Forgive me. Forgive me."

Jamie had drifted off to sleep, and Adam still hadn't returned. Maybe he'd gone home. He'd clearly been uncomfortable here, making her wonder why he'd stayed at all.

Because he cares. The thought slipped into her mind and wouldn't be dismissed. If he cared…

Well, if he cared, he'd have come back. And he hadn't, so that was her answer. She walked to the window and stood staring out at the dark rooftops and the dim reflection of lights from the parking lot. She didn't want Adam to feel responsible for them, so it was ridiculous to be disappointed when he didn't.

When she stopped focusing on the distant parking lot, the window became a mirror. It reflected the high hospital bed, the array of monitors, the glow of a sensor light here and there. Her own face, looking drawn and tired.

And the door, which swung inward as she watched. She turned.

"I thought you'd left." She didn't mean that to sound accusing. Had it?

Adam shook his head. Standing just inside the door he was in shadow, but she could see the movement.

"Did you get your coffee?" She took a step toward him, disturbed by his odd stillness.

"No." His voice sounded raw. "I went to the chapel instead."

"I see." But she didn't. Something was bothering him. Maybe just being here. Sitting with a sick child wasn't for everyone. "If you want to leave now…"

"I have to tell you something." He moved forward, until the shaded light from above the bed touched him.

Her breath caught. He looked distraught. Emotionally drained, his eyes red as if he'd been crying.

That shocked her down to her soles. Adam wouldn't cry—not strong, self-controlled Adam.

"I have to tell you something," he said again and stood looking at her as if asking for permission.

She didn't want to hear it. That was her first thought. Whatever had the power to make Adam look like that, she didn't want to hear.

But that would be cowardly. She pulled the pair of chairs away from the bed a little. "Come. Sit down."

He nodded, moving to sit down next to her. "I want you to know that I'm not as perfect as you seem to think." He tried to smile, but it came out more like a grimace.

"Adam…" It distressed her, seeing him this way. "You look exhausted. Maybe you should put this off until tomorrow."

And maybe by then he'd have decided to keep whatever it was to himself. She didn't necessarily want that, but she also didn't want him to tell her something in the stress of the moment and then regret it afterward.

"I'm not going to sleep until I get this off my chest. It's something—" He stopped, then started again. "Something that happened when I was stationed in Miami."

Something must have happened when Adam was in south Florida. Georgia's voice echoed in her mind. *He won't talk about it, but I know it affected him.*

Georgia had said maybe he'd tell her. Had asked her to listen.

"Tell me," she said softly, knowing she didn't have a choice.

"We had gone out on a routine patrol, fairly far out." His voice was gravelly, as if he hadn't used it in a while. "We spotted a boat that we thought was smugglers."

She nodded. His father had talked about the smugglers, and Benny had mentioned them, too.

"We headed for the boat to check it out. It was riding low in the water. I can see it now, so I must have seen it then. I must have wondered." His hands gripped the arms of the chair. "When they spotted us, they started to make a run for it."

He stopped, as if he'd run out of steam.

"So you chased them," she suggested.

He nodded. "We called to them over the horn. Identified ourselves, told them to pull up. When they didn't respond, the next thing to do was fire a shot in front of them. That's the procedure."

He seemed to be arguing with himself about it, or maybe he just wanted to be sure she understood. She nodded.

He swallowed, and she could see the muscles work in his neck. "I gave the order. When we fired, the pilot tried to pull the boat around. I don't know what he thought he was doing. Just panicked, maybe." The flow of words came faster now, as if he wanted to get to the end of it. "She couldn't take the turn he tried to put her into. A wave hit, swamping them. All in an instant, she capsized, and we saw why she rode so low in the water." He swallowed again, his face so drawn that he looked old and ill. "People. Illegals, running from Cuba, we found out later. Thirty-five of them, crammed on a boat that shouldn't have carried half that many, hiding under a tarp on deck. The water was full of them. Screams, crying. For an instant we were so shocked I don't think we reacted at all."

"You tried to save them."

"We didn't have room for them all on the patrol boat. Took the ones who were weakest or injured first, called for help." He drove his fingers through his hair, as if he'd pull the images from his brain. "I spotted a kid…a little boy about Jamie's age. A piece of metal had been driven into his side somehow when they went over. His mother was trying to hold him up, and the water around them was red with blood."

"Dear God." It was all she could say.

"I went in after him. Got him out. We got him to the hospital, finally, in Miami."

She tried not to imagine that frantic scene. "Was he all right? The rest of them?"

"We got them all, eventually. The little boy—his name was Juan. They had to operate to get the metal out."

"Was he all right?"

"He lost a lot of blood, but they were in time." He shook his head. "I went with them to the hospital. Waited with the mother. She was so terrified."

"Yes," she whispered. She knew how that was. How terrifying to have your child in pain, in danger, and be able to do nothing. "No wonder you hate hospitals."

"It was my fault, you see." He went on as if she hadn't spoken. "I should have seen the boat was overloaded. I should have realized what was going on. It was my fault."

She forced herself to think past the horror of what had happened. "Is that what your commander thought?"

He shook his head. "I followed the rules. As far as the Coast Guard is concerned, I didn't do anything wrong. But I'm responsible."

"No." She reached out to put her hand over his. He gripped the arm of the chair so tightly it seemed she could feel every separate muscle straining. "Adam, you can't think that. Of course it was terrible, but you weren't to blame."

His eyes were dark, his gaze inward. He couldn't be absolved so easily.

"What happened to the little boy?" Her heart crunched, thinking of Jamie.

"I went to see him in the hospital every day. He was getting better. I'd take him some little toy when I went in." His lips twitched. "I thought—I wanted to help. But one day the room was empty. They'd been sent back to Cuba. I never heard anything of them again."

She wanted to cry at the despair in his voice, but that wouldn't do Adam any good. "Adam, I know you feel responsible. That's in your nature." That was the kind of honorable man he was. "But you did everything you could."

"I've been telling myself that for over a year. And then, when I saw Jamie, it all came back. That look of suffering—Juan looked like that." He shook his head. "I can't lock it away anymore. That's what I was doing in the chapel. Confessing. Trying to be honest about it with God."

She held his hand and spoke what she believed to be the truth. "Whatever you did or didn't do, if you've confessed it, God has already forgiven you. Now you have to accept that forgiveness."

"You really think it's that easy?" His gaze met hers.

"I don't think it's easy at all." She thought of the wrongs she'd had to confess. "But you have to, if you're ever going to be over it."

He nodded slowly, his hand turning to clasp hers. "Thank you, Cathy. I don't know if I can, but thank you."

She tried to smile. Tried to think only of his pain, not her own.

But one thing was very clear to her now. Adam's feelings for Jamie and for her weren't real. They couldn't be. He was substituting Jamie for that boy he thought he'd failed. And no one could build a relationship on that.

Chapter Fifteen

Three days had passed since Jamie's surgery—three days that had become a blur, scenes blending into one another, the hospital routine superimposed over the natural order of day and night.

She hurried through the lobby, clutching the bag with some books and toys Jamie had wanted brought from the beach house. She hadn't wanted to leave him, but Miz Callie had insisted Cathy needed a break. Cathy could take her car, and she'd stay with Jamie.

She hurried toward the elevators. The huge hospital, which had seemed such a confusing maze at first, was now as familiar as Miz Callie's house. She passed the gift shop and stopped at the sight of Miz Callie emerging, holding a white plastic bag with a package of red licorice sticking out the top.

She shook her head, smiling. "You shouldn't have let Jamie talk you into that."

Miz Callie looked just a little embarrassed. "He said it was his favorite candy, bless him. If you can't have your favorite candy when you're recuperating, when can you? I was just so happy he has his appetite back, I'd have gotten him about anything."

"Still, he shouldn't be asking for things." Jamie was getting used to a life where you didn't have to count every penny.

"You were supposed to eat lunch and take a little nap before you came back." Miz Callie fixed her with a stern gaze. "I don't suppose for a minute you did either of those things."

Her gaze slid away from Miz Callie's. "I'll get something from the vending machine later."

"No, you will not." Miz Callie took her arm. "You'll go right into the cafeteria with me and eat something decent, and I'm going to watch you while you do it."

"I can't. Jamie—"

"Jamie's fine. Adam is with him, and he's perfectly happy. You just come along with me."

If Jamie had been alone, she'd never have given in. But Adam was there, and no doubt Miz Callie was right. Jamie was happy. More to the point, she didn't want to see Adam.

"All right," she said, giving in to the pressure of

Miz Callie's hand on her arm. "But I don't want more than a sandwich. Really."

The cafeteria held a smattering of people, as it always did—folks whose ordinary lives were, like hers, temporarily changed, governed by hospital rules and hospital schedules. She grabbed a tray and pushed it along the rack.

Nothing looked very appealing, but she took a tuna sandwich to please Miz Callie, and added a glass of sweet tea.

Miz Callie took a glass of tea for herself, and then she added a dish of tapioca pudding to Cathy's tray. "Just try it," she said. "Pudding slides down easy when you're feeling tense."

"Not tense, exactly," she said once they'd paid and found a table. "Just—well, I'll do better once Jamie is home."

Except that he wouldn't be home, not really. He'd be going back to Miz Callie's place. Miz Callie and Grandpa seemed to have settled that between them, and she hadn't been able to argue, despite her feeling that having a convalescent child around might be a bit much for Miz Callie.

But where else would they go? She'd have the same feeling of imposing if they went back to Adam's parents' house, and Jamie had to stay in Charleston at least until his six weeks of therapy were finished. Then…well, then she didn't know.

Miz Callie patted her hand. "Don't worry so

much, child. It's going to work out. Of course you'll feel better when you have Jamie home again. My land, I remember when Adam and Cole had their tonsils out at the same time. They both needed it, and Delia figured having them both done at once was the easiest way to get Cole to behave, having his older brother there to set a good example."

Yet another time when his family depended on Adam to be the perfect one. No wonder he took it so hard when he felt he'd failed.

"Did it work?"

"Well, Adam was good as gold, of course. Cole ran us all a merry chase, trying to keep him still." Miz Callie shook her head, smiling at the memory. "You ask Georgia. Poor Georgia played one video game after another with him, even though she hated it."

Shared memories, she thought. Those shared memories were part of what made the Bodines so close. No matter how welcome they made her, she would never have that.

"Is somethin' going on with that grandson of mine? Did he upset you?"

"No. Adam…he's been so helpful." She couldn't meet Miz Callie's bright blue gaze. Adam had told her something he hadn't told his family.

Why hadn't he talked to them about it? Was it because of this image they all had of Adam as the strong one? Maybe he couldn't bear to have them look at him differently.

As for her... Well, he'd told her because... She groped toward an understanding. In Adam's mind, Jamie was all mixed up with that other boy, the one who caused his guilt. The one he hadn't been able to help.

Adam's inner torment and his outer world were colliding, and she couldn't help him. Her heart twisted, and her stomach rebelled at the thought of one more bit of tuna. She put the sandwich down.

"That's all I can eat. I should get back to Jamie."

Miz Callie took her hand again, stopping her as she rose. "It's obvious that something's gone wrong between you and Adam. I had hoped... Well, never mind. Just know that I love you and Jamie, no matter what."

Her throat was too tight for speech. She could only nod.

"Good." Miz Callie stood. "Now, I'm going to cut along home and bake some cookies. The doctor's going to let our boy come home soon, and I want a full cookie jar to greet him."

That made her smile. Miz Callie had a firm conviction that love and cookies cured most of childhood's ills, and maybe she had a point.

That thought comforted her all the way up to Jamie's room. She pushed open the door and stopped. Jamie and Adam were bent over a game board, heads close together, laughing. Her heart seemed to stop for a moment and then resume thudding with a faster beat, sounding the inevitable truth that she couldn't deny any longer. She loved Adam. It was futile, it was useless, but she loved him.

"So anyway, it looks like Uncle Ned paid off the store owner and the charges against Cathy were dropped," Hugh said.

Adam nodded. Hugh had caught him just going off duty, and they stood in the parking lot, leaning against Hugh's car, to talk.

"I know."

Hugh gave him a sideways glance. "You know. How do you know? I just finally got through to someone with answers this morning."

"I talked to Cathy about it." *Confronted* would be a better word. He'd forced her to relive something she'd thought safely buried in the past. His mind winced. There was a lot of that going around.

"I thought we were going to hold off until I got the info." Hugh was mildly accusing.

"Yeah, well…" He shrugged. "I shouldn't have said anything, I guess. But we were disagreeing about something, and it sort of came out."

"You'd make a lousy interrogator."

"Good thing that's not my job," he said. "Anyway,

it doesn't much matter. We know the truth of it now. She was desperately afraid for a sick child. That doesn't make it right, but I can put myself in her shoes."

"They've had a rough time of it." Hugh leaned back against the car, folding his arms, apparently not bothered by the hot metal. "Funny, the turns life takes. If Uncle Ned hadn't fought with his father, maybe they'd have always been part of our lives."

"If," Adam repeated. "If he hadn't fought with his father, maybe he'd never have met Cathy's grandmother. Like Miz Callie says, you can't change the past."

He took a look at the words as soon as he'd spoken them, confused for a moment. That wasn't what he was trying to do, was it?

"You're gettin' right fond of her, aren't you?" Hugh drawled.

What was he made of anymore? Glass?

"I guess." He shook his head at Hugh's demanding gaze. "Don't look at me like that. It's complicated."

"What's complicated about it? You like her, she likes you, you see where it goes."

"If it were that easy—" He stopped, glared at his cousin. "For one thing, she's completely wrapped up in taking care of Jamie right now. You can't expect her to be thinking about anything else. And for another, I'm not so sure I'm ready for anything serious."

"Why not? As my mama keeps reminding me, we're not getting any younger. And since you're four months older than me, I figure you've got to take the plunge first."

"It's not a matter of age." It was a question of doubting yourself.

Hugh stared at him for a long moment—the kind of stare that probably had the bad guys tripping over themselves to confess all. "This have something to do with what happened to you down in Florida?"

Adam could only stare at him. "You mean... How do you know about that?"

He shrugged. "Coast Guard's a small world. Word gets around. And I know you, so I knew how you'd be feeling about it. How you'd be figuring you had to be to blame."

"I was," he said shortly. He didn't need Hugh lecturing him. It was bad enough that he knew. Did everyone else? No one had said a word about it. Maybe they were waiting for him to bring it up.

"I knew you'd be trying to take too much on yourself." Hugh sounded gloomy at having been proved right. "Look, the jerks who soaked those poor people of every dime and then crammed them on an unsafe boat—they're the bad guys here, not you."

"You think I don't know that?" he flared. "But if I hadn't ordered that warning shot, the boat might not have capsized."

"Yeah, and it might have capsized out at sea with no one around to pick up the survivors. Ever think of that?" Hugh shoved himself away from the car. "Sure, you're responsible, just like we're all responsible for every life at risk out there." He jerked his head toward the ocean. "That's what we signed on for. Responsible, yes, but not to blame."

Cathy had tried to say something equally comforting, but she didn't know what it was like. Hugh did. He tried to get a grip on the thoughts that were spinning in his head.

"Don't you have any doubts?" He blurted the question before he could stop himself. "Don't you ever wonder if you're going to fail someone?"

The lines in Hugh's face seemed to deepen. He rubbed his hand along his bad leg. "'Course I wonder. I wonder what'll happen if they ever let me get back where I belong. Will I second-guess myself the next time I'm approaching a suspect vessel? Maybe. I figure all I can do is my duty, and hope that's enough. We hold people's lives in our hands out there, but we're not God. That's somethin' to remember."

More than remember, Adam thought as he waved goodbye to his cousin and drove to the medical center. Words to live by, maybe. He tried to adjust to a different way of looking at what had happened. Maybe Hugh was right. And if he was…

He was still trying to figure out what that meant for him when he walked down the hall to Jamie's room. He hadn't told Cathy he'd be stopping by, but she ought to be used to it by now.

He pushed open the door and went spiraling back into the past. The room was empty. Jamie was gone.

Cathy went down the stairs from the house to the car. Several bags hadn't been brought in yet, and now that Jamie was napping, worn out from the excitement of coming home from the hospital, she could take care of them.

She paused, hand on the railing, her thoughts turning inward. She'd been so caught up in the moment that she hadn't had time to think about what this meant. Now she did, and her heart overflowed with joy and praise.

Thank You, dear Lord. Thank You for opening this door to a better life for my son. He's going to be whole.

Tears stung her eyes. Jamie would be as strong and healthy as any other boy his age. He'd have weeks and weeks of therapy, but eventually all this would be in the past. A year from now, he'd probably barely remember a time when he couldn't do what other children did.

I am so thankful, Father. I know now that it was Your hand that brought us here. You never stopped guiding us and caring for us, even during those years when I doubted. Please, continue to show me the path You have for me.

She would try hard not to long for something she couldn't have. That would be ungrateful. If she'd dreamed of something more with Adam—well, now she understood that it wasn't to be.

She went on down the stairs and opened the trunk of the car. Three plastic bags stuffed with books and toys remained, all of them things that this unexpected new family of theirs had lavished on Jamie in the hospital. More toys that he'd ever received in this life, in fact, and just the thought made the tears well up again.

Foolish, she scolded herself. Her emotions were too close to the surface these days. Natural enough, but she needed to get control of herself. There would be difficult days again, no doubt, days when Jamie rebelled at the pain of therapy, times when he cried or was angry. She had to be strong then.

Adam would know how to urge Jamie through those times. That treacherous little voice in the back of her mind wouldn't be still. *Jamie would do anything Adam wanted him to.*

But she wasn't going to rely on Adam. He had...

That thought slipped away as a car pulled up

in front of her. Adam's car, stopping in a spray of crushed shell that was probably an eloquent statement of his mood.

She stood where she was, her heart hammering against her ribs, as he slammed his way out of the car and advanced on her, his expression thunderous.

"Jamie's home?"

At her nod, his face tightened even more. "Why didn't you tell me? I got to the hospital, and when he wasn't there—" His mouth clamped shut on the words, his eyes bleak.

She understood then, and her heart cramped. He'd relived the past. Adam had walked into an empty hospital room, and he'd experienced again what he had before, the symbol of what he considered his failure.

"I'm sorry." Her voice trembled on the words. She wanted to touch him, to put a comforting hand on his, but she didn't dare. "I didn't think. I intended to call you once you were off duty. I'm sorry."

"You should have called." He bit the words off. "I'd have come and helped you bring Jamie home."

"I know. I'm sorry." Her heart twisted a bit more. He'd have come, out of his sense of responsibility and guilt. "Your father helped us."

"You should have called me," he said again. Then he blew out a breath, seeming to try to rid himself of his frustration. "Okay. Sorry. I thought Jamie wasn't being released until tomorrow at the earliest."

"That's what I thought, too." She could breathe again. The storm seemed to have passed. "But when the doctor visited this morning, he was so pleased that he decided to let him go today."

"Good, good." He seemed almost distracted, as if he struggled with something deep beneath the surface. "How did he handle the trip home?"

"Excited." She had to smile, remembering Jamie's exuberance when they'd crossed the drawbridge onto the island. "I thought we'd never get him to settle down, but he's finally taking a nap." She gestured toward the bags in the trunk. "This is the first chance I've had to finish unloading."

Normal, nice and normal, she told herself. *Keep things on the surface, and it won't hurt so much.* She reached for one of the bags.

He clasped her hand, stopping her. His touch seemed to shimmer along her skin and stop her breath.

"Leave it for a minute. There's something I want to say to you."

She nodded, praying that her cheeks hadn't flushed, giving away her reaction to his hand warm on hers. "What is it?"

A muscle in his jaw jumped with tension, and his

grip tightened. "Cathy…" He took a ragged breath. "I think you should marry me."

She'd heard him wrong. He couldn't have said what she thought he'd said. She stared at him.

His brows came down. "Did you hear me? I said I think we should get married."

Her heart was performing some wild acrobatics as joy flooded through her. Everything she'd wanted…

I think we should get married, he'd said. Not *I love you, Cathy.*

If she looked into his eyes, she'd know. She forced herself to look at him. "Why?"

He was taken aback. "What do you mean, why? Why does anybody get married? We care about each other—we both know that. You know how fond I am of Jamie, and I think he likes me. We could be a family. As my dependent, all of his medical care would be covered by the military. You'd never have to worry about that again. You'd be here, with family, where you belong."

He was giving her reasons. Too many reasons. Every one but the right one. The joy seeped slowly away, leaving an acrid taste behind.

She could say yes. The word was there, on the tip of her tongue. She could make do with whatever love Adam had to offer. He'd be a good father, and at least—

"No." The word was out before she finished rationalizing. "I can't."

Whatever he'd expected, it wasn't that. He stared at her, his eyes darkening. "I guess it's my turn to ask why." His voice was tightly controlled. "I thought we had something."

"I thought we did, too." She had to hang on to her control long enough to say this. She could cry later, when she was alone. "But it's not enough. When we came here…" She stopped, took a breath, calmed her shaking voice. "When we came here, I wouldn't have dreamed this could happen. If I had dreamed it, I'd have known it was all I wanted."

"Well, then…"

She shook her head. "You aren't offering your whole heart, Adam. We both know that. Jamie and I are all tangled up in your thoughts with that other child." She tried to swallow the lump in her throat before it choked her off entirely. "Once that would have been enough. I thought love was always conditional. Grandpa would love me if I fulfilled his dreams for me. My husband would have loved me if I'd produced a perfect child."

She did choke up then. He looked as if he'd burst into speech, and she held up her hand to stop him.

"I've found my way back since then. Back to God, back to an understanding of what He has for

me. I love you, Adam, with all my heart. I can't
settle for less than that in return."

He stared at her for a long moment. If he spoke,
if he said he loved her that way…

He turned. He walked away.

She watched him, dry-eyed, until his car was of
out of sight. Then she leaned against the railing,
clinging to it as if she were very old.

She'd had to do it. She and Jamie would be
all right. But she'd be a long time getting over
Adam.

Chapter Sixteen

It had been nearly a week since Adam had seen Cathy alone. He braced himself against the rail of the patrol boat, sweeping the area with binoculars. Nothing there but a lot of empty ocean.

He'd made an effort to be sure there were plenty of other people around when he went to visit Jamie. Brave little kid—Adam's heart had wrenched a few times, watching him when the therapist made a home visit. Jamie had to struggle to do everything the therapist said, but he always had a smile on his face at the end of a visit.

As for Cathy—well, all Adam could do was make an effort to keep the situation from being uncomfortable for her. He'd tried being angry with her, but that hadn't worked, mainly because he'd recognized the truth in the things she'd said.

He'd been trying to fake his commitment. No wonder she'd turned him down. Not out of pride;

he couldn't accuse her of that. She'd discovered her true worth in God's sight in recent weeks, and he had to honor that.

The truth was that he was disgusted with himself. He lowered the glasses, balancing easily on the moving deck. For the past year he'd been ignoring what he felt, suppressing his guilt, only letting it come out in the occasional nightmare. And then Cathy and Jamie had come into his life, and the feelings had burst free.

That was God's doing, he supposed, introducing him to the one woman in the world who had the power to make him see the truth about himself.

He'd thought, that night in the hospital chapel, that he'd gotten past his feelings. But then he'd rushed into trying to fill the hole in his heart by asking Cathy to marry him in that way.

She'd been right to turn away from him, but wrong about one thing. He did love her. His heart ached with it. But his feelings for her were still hampered by his own doubts.

Give me a clear eye, Lord. Let me see who I really am.

He recognized it then, and wondered how long he'd been staring at it. A boat, off to the southeast. He shifted into duty mode.

He looked at Terry and pointed. Terry nodded, beginning the wide arc that would put them on an intercept course.

"They've seen us," Jim said, raising his voice above the engine noise.

For a moment it hung in the balance. Then the other boat surged forward, turning toward open ocean.

None of them needed explanations or orders. They went into pursuit mode automatically, closing the distance between them and the fleeing vessel rapidly. Jim readied weapons while Terry manned the loudspeaker.

Adam kept his glasses on the other boat. "They're underpowered and overloaded." His glasses swept over a large tarp that could be shielding almost anything. He eyed it coolly, watching for movement. Nothing.

He focused on the crew. Five of them that he could see, and—"They're armed," he said. "Radio for assistance."

Jim shoved a weapon into his hands. He took it, almost able to feel Jim's adrenaline pumping. As for himself—his mind ticked over possibilities, assessing them. No thrill of the chase, no apprehension of its outcome. Just do your duty.

Hugh's words flicked in his mind. *We hold lives in our hands, but we're not God. Do your duty. That's all you can ask of yourself. Leave the rest in God's capable hands.*

"Fire a warning shot."

For an instant he thought they'd keep running.

Then the boat's speed slackened. A couple of small black objects arced into the sea and disappeared.

"Getting rid of their cell phones," Jim growled. "Smugglers are getting too smart."

"Smart enough to know we'd trace their buddies, anyway." He kept his focus on the men's hands as they came alongside, watching for movement toward weapons.

Nothing, and in a moment they'd boarded. Adam approached the tarp, alert for movement. He grasped the edge and threw it back. Wooden packing crates, but not cigarettes this time. Weapons. He and Jim swung around as one, their own weapons at the ready.

The bigger the reward for the smugglers, the more readiness to take a risk. He spotted one man's hand moving toward his belt even as the thought entered his mind, and he snarled a command in Spanish.

For an instant his finger was taut on the trigger. Then the man lifted his hands in the air, and he could breathe again.

By the time all five smugglers had been secured and their ambitious cargo inspected, a cutter was bearing down on them.

"Might know somebody else would show up to bag all the glory," Jim muttered, watching as their prisoners were herded on board the larger vessel.

Adam grinned at him, feeling remarkably

relaxed. "Come on, hero. We don't need glory. Just doing what they pay us for."

Jim snorted. "Duty. That all you ever think about?"

"Not all."

He'd asked God for a clear eye, and that had been granted. A clear eye to do his duty. And now, it seemed, a clear enough eye to see what he needed to tell Cathy.

Cathy sat on a towel at the edge of a tidal pool, looking with profound pleasure and thankfulness at Jamie, splashing in the pool. Don, the home health therapist who came every other day, had said that, now that Jamie's stitches were out, exercising in the warm water was the best thing for him.

Cathy's gratitude seemed to know no boundaries, including Don, with his gruff voice and gentle hands; Grandpa, with his seemingly endless fund of stories about his childhood keeping Jamie amused; Miz Callie, cooking anything she thought Jamie might like; the rest of the family, with their cheerful attention. Even the warm October sun and gentle waves seemed designed especially to help Jamie heal.

With so much to be grateful for, she'd discovered that after a week, she could sometimes go for as long as five minutes without thinking of Adam and mourning what she'd lost. That was progress, wasn't it?

Keep me focused on gratitude, dear Father. Remind me to trust in You.

"Mama?" Jamie studied his toes, poking out of the water. "Am I going to go to Lindsay's school? Don said I'd be ready to go back to school in a month maybe, and I said I didn't go to school, but since I'm six, I could."

"I don't know, sugar. We'll have to think about that." The question was a small jolt, reminding her that they couldn't stay in this pleasant cocoon forever. Sooner or later, they had to go back to their real lives. Easier lives, thanks to Miz Callie's insistence on Grandpa taking a share of his father's estate, but still…

Isolated. That was the word she groped for. In such a short time, she'd grown accustomed to the idea of family. She drew a circle idly in the sand with a shell, then connected it to a series of other circles. Connectedness. It had been missing in their lives before, and now that she'd tasted it, she didn't want to do without it.

When they left, she wouldn't have the constant reminders of Adam. You'd think that would make her happy, but her stubborn heart didn't seem very logical, longing for him even though just a glimpse made the pain worse.

"Jamie, look. Dolphins." She pointed to the sea.

"Where, Mama? I missed them."

Bless his heart, he always seemed to just miss seeing the dolphins. "Watch right there, just past where that pelican is, see? Keep watching, and maybe they'll come up again. There were two of them."

"I don't see," he began, and then interrupted himself with a squeal. "I see them! Mama, I see them."

"Good job, Jamie." She reached out to pat his hair, wet where he'd splashed himself.

He turned, giving her a grin that could only be called mischievous. "I see something else, Mama. Guess what?"

"A seagull?" she asked, delighted at his playfulness. "A sandpiper?"

"Wrong!" he said. "It's Adam!"

She looked in the direction he pointed, her heart lurching. Adam came toward them across the sand, and in that instant she knew that it was no use trying to forget him. She'd learn to live with it, but she'd never forget anything about him…especially not the way his eyes warmed when he smiled at her son.

"Hey, Jamie. Look at you, in the water again."

"I'm allowed now," Jamie said proudly. "Don said so."

Adam sat down next to her. "Don?" he asked.

"Don is the physical therapist, remember?" She tried to keep her voice even, tried to still the pulse that pounded through her with the awareness of his arm brushing hers.

"Don says I can swim." Jamie stretched skinny legs out behind him, planting his hands on the sandy bottom. "See?" He crawled across the pool.

"Good going, Jamie." He lowered his voice. "It sounds as if I've been replaced in Jamie's esteem by Don the therapist."

"That could never happen," she said, and knew it to be true. No one could replace Adam in Jamie's eyes. Adam had, in such a short period of time, become indispensable to her son's happiness.

Isn't that enough? Some part of her asked the question. *People have built a marriage on less.*

"You were right." Adam said the words abruptly. "You were right last week, when you turned me down."

She couldn't speak, because grief had a stranglehold on her throat. She could only nod. That was it, then. He'd recognized for himself how impossible it was.

"I've been doing a lot of thinking since then. And praying." Adam linked his hands around his knees. Long fingers entwined. It should have been a relaxed posture, but it wasn't. The muscles in his forearms were taut cords.

"You asked me once why I always had to be the perfect one," he said. "The responsible one, the guy everybody turned to." His shoulders moved. "I can't say I know that—it's just how I'm made. But when that business happened down in the Keys…" He broke off for a moment, then continued. "I doubted myself then. I couldn't find that conviction anymore. So I tried to fake it. Tried to push the memories out of sight and go on as if nothing had happened. I was getting pretty good at that, too, except for the nightmares. Until I met you."

She felt him shift, knew he was studying her face.

"For whatever reason, you had the power to make me face it, Cathy."

"Because we reminded you of that boy and his mother." Her voice rasped, on the edge of tears.

"Maybe so. But I think now it was what God planned all along. Something had to force me to come clean with God. With myself. That something was you." He moved, his hand covering hers. "Cathy, don't you see? It isn't that I care for you because you remind me of them. What happened out there humbled me. It made me recognize that I'm a flawed human being who needs someone else to make him whole. And you're that someone for me." He lifted her hand, holding it between both of his. "You were right to turn me down before, but you'd be wrong to do it now. I know my heart, and I offer it to you without reservations. I love you, Cathy. Won't you at least look at me?"

She lifted her gaze, half-afraid to see what was written in his face. But she saw tranquility there she hadn't seen before, and his eyes were filled with love. For her.

Her heart seemed to leap, like one of the dolphins arcing from the water. Adam was saying the truth, and loving each other was what they were meant to do for a lifetime.

She found her voice. "Yes," she said. "I'm saying yes."

Adam stood in the October sunshine on the tiny barrier island where Miz Callie's nature preserve was being dedicated at last. Cathy was on one side of him, while Jamie pressed close on the other. A surge of overwhelming gratitude went through him, strong as a storm tide.

When Cathy said yes to him, he'd thought he'd loved her as much as it was humanly possible to love. He'd realized since how foolish that was—each day their love grew stronger and surer. In thirty years they'd be like his parents, knowing each other so well that they often had no need for words. And in sixty—well, they'd be together forever, even as Miz Callie was still connected to Granddad.

He rested his hand on Jamie's shoulder. His love

for Jamie, too, couldn't be stronger if he were the boy's biological father. Perhaps he and Cathy would have more children, perhaps not, but Jamie would always be his son.

Miz Callie was speaking now to the assembled crowd, her blue eyes snapping with her usual enthusiasm, her face alight with pleasure at this fulfillment of her dream. Most of the people here were family, but small groups had come from various veterans' organizations, led by Uncle Ned's old friend, Benny. Active-duty personnel were there, too, representing all the military installations in the greater Charleston area.

For the most part, though, this was a family time. Georgia and Matt with their Lindsay, his cousin Amanda and her fiancé, Trent, Adam's parents, his aunts and uncles, and all the Bodine cousins—even his brother Cole had wangled enough leave to get home for this event. Cole, like the others, would come home to stay eventually, he was sure of it. Like all the Bodines, this place was in his blood.

"This began simply," Miz Callie was saying. "With my memories of the past and the need to right an old wrong. It has brought us far more than we ever imagined. It has restored our family."

Adam's hand found Cathy's. Miz Callie's quest had brought him more than he'd ever have dreamed, too.

"I wanted to name this preserve for my husband's

brother, Edward Bodine." Miz Callie glanced at Uncle Ned, standing next to her. "But Ned had other ideas. And so…"

She reached out to pull the covering from the simple stone marker with its brass plaque. "Patriot's Preserve," she said, her clear voice trembling slightly. "This nature sanctuary is dedicated in honor of all the courageous men and women of the lowcountry who have served and continue to serve their country." She wiped away a tear.

"Amen," he murmured softly. "Amen."

* * * * *

Dear Reader,

Thank you for choosing to pick up the third book in my new Love Inspired series about the Bodine family of South Carolina. I am really enjoying writing about the Bodines, and the more I uncover about the family, the more I want to write.

Adam has appeared in the other two books in the series, so he was really calling for his own story. It wasn't easy to find the vulnerability in such a strong character, but I hope you'll feel he met his match in Cathy and her little boy.

I hope you'll let me know how you felt about this story, and I'd love to send you a signed bookmark or my brochure of Pennsylvania Dutch recipes. You can write to me at Steeple Hill Books, 233 Broadway, Suite 1001, New York, NY 10279, e-mail me at marta@martaperry.com, or visit me on the web at www.martaperry.com.

Blessings,

Marta Perry

QUESTIONS FOR DISCUSSION

1. Can you understand why Adam was troubled by doubts about himself after the incident with the overloaded boat? What do you think he should have done to resolve those feelings?

2. Adam's personality makes him take responsibility in every situation. Is that always a good reaction? Can you think of a time in which that might backfire on a person?

3. Cathy struggles with her sense that she has failed to live up to the expectations people had of her. Has this ever happened to you? How do you sort out God's calling from the demands of others?

4. Cathy's grandfather is so caught up in his anger over what happened to him in the past that he can't see his present clearly. How do you deal with it when you can't forget a hurt?

5. Cathy's faith faltered after her child was born with a disability. Have you ever experienced that? If so, how did you come back to God?

6. The scripture verse for this story reminds us that we must forgive if we're going to be

forgiven. How do you feel about doing that? Is it difficult to do that in the press of your daily life and experiences?

7. Cathy finds it difficult to face the situation she finds herself in, but she has to find the courage for the sake of her son. Have you ever found you're able to do things for others that you couldn't for yourself?

8. Why do you think Cathy was so antagonistic to Adam at first? What was she afraid of? Did you understand her feelings, even if you didn't agree?

9. Adam's grandmother longs to find the truth about the past. Do you think it's always a good idea to do that?

10. Did you sympathize with Cathy's grandfather's fears and his reaction to them? How might he have handled the situation better?

11. In the end, Cathy's grandfather realizes that he is treating her in the same unforgiving way that his father treated him. Why was it so difficult for him to see that?

12. Cathy realizes that in the bad times, all she has to cling to is God. Do you think God can use

the difficulties we encounter to help us to turn to Him? Has that ever happened to you?

13. Which character in the story did you feel was living the most Christlike life? Why?

14. How did you feel about Cathy's reactions when Adam told her the story of the injured child? Do you think she should have reacted differently?

15. In the end, with God's help, Cathy and Adam and Cathy's grandfather have discovered the meaning of forgiveness—in forgiving others, asking God's forgiveness and forgiving themselves. Which of these do you think is the most difficult?

LARGER-PRINT BOOKS!

**GET 2 FREE
LARGER-PRINT NOVELS
PLUS 2 FREE
MYSTERY GIFTS**

Larger-print novels are now available...

YES! Please send me 2 FREE LARGER-PRINT Love Inspired® novels and my 2 FREE mystery gifts (gifts are worth about $10). After receiving them, if I don't wish to receive any more books, I can return the shipping statement marked "cancel". If I don't cancel, I will receive 6 brand-new novels every month and be billed just $4.74 per book in the U.S. or $5.24 per book in Canada. That's a saving of over 20% off the cover price. It's quite a bargain! Shipping and handling is just 50¢ per book.* I understand that accepting the 2 free books and gifts places me under no obligation to buy anything. I can always return a shipment and cancel at any time. Even if I never buy another book, the two free books and gifts are mine to keep forever.

122/322 IDN E7QP

Name _____ (PLEASE PRINT) _____

Address _____ Apt. #

City _____ State/Prov. _____ Zip/Postal Code

Signature (if under 18, a parent or guardian must sign)

Mail to Steeple Hill Reader Service:
**IN U.S.A.: P.O. Box 1867, Buffalo, NY 14240-1867
IN CANADA: P.O. Box 609, Fort Erie, Ontario L2A 5X3**

Not valid to current subscribers to Love Inspired Larger-Print books.

**Are you a current subscriber to Love Inspired books
and want to receive the larger-print edition?
Call 1-800-873-8635 or visit www.morefreebooks.com.**

* Terms and prices subject to change without notice. Prices do not include applicable taxes. Sales tax applicable in N.Y. Canadian residents will be charged applicable provincial taxes and GST. Offer not valid in Quebec. This offer is limited to one order per household. All orders subject to approval. Credit or debit balances in a customer's account(s) may be offset by any other outstanding balance owed by or to the customer. Please allow 4 to 6 weeks for delivery. Offer available while quantities last.

Your Privacy: Steeple Hill Books is committed to protecting your privacy. Our Privacy Policy is available online at www.SteepleHill.com or upon request from the Reader Service. From time to time we make our lists of customers available to reputable third parties who may have a product or service of interest to you. If you would prefer we not share your name and address, please check here. ☐

Help us get it right—We strive for accurate, respectful and relevant communications. To clarify or modify your communication preferences, visit us at www.ReaderService.com/consumerschoice.

LILP10R

Love Inspired ®
SUSPENSE
RIVETING INSPIRATIONAL ROMANCE

Watch for our new series of
edge-of-your-seat suspense novels.
These contemporary tales
of intrigue and romance
feature Christian characters
facing challenges to their faith...
and their lives!

NOW AVAILABLE IN REGULAR
& LARGER-PRINT FORMATS

Steeple
Hill ®

Visit:
www.SteepleHill.com

LISUSDIR10

Love Inspired. HISTORICAL

INSPIRATIONAL HISTORICAL ROMANCE

Engaging stories of romance,
adventure and faith,
these novels are set in
various historical periods
from biblical times
to World War II.

NOW AVAILABLE!

**Steeple
Hill®**